Redeemed Hearts

Susan Anne Mason

This is a work of fiction. Names, characters, places, and incidents either are the product of the author's imagination or are used fictitiously, and any resemblance to actual persons living or dead, business establishments, events, or locales, is entirely coincidental.

Redeemed Hearts

COPYRIGHT 2016 by Susan Anne Mason

Contact Information: titleadmin@pelicanbookgroup.com

All scripture quotations, unless otherwise indicated, are taken from the Holy Bible, New International Version(R) NIV(R) Copyright 1973, 1978, 1984, 2011 by Biblica, Inc.™ Used by permission of Zondervan. All rights reserved worldwide. www.zondervan.com

Cover Art by *Nicola Martinez*

White Rose Publishing, a division of Pelican Ventures, LLC
www.pelicanbookgroup.com PO Box 1738 *Aztec, NM * 87410

White Rose Publishing Circle and Rosebud logo is a trademark of Pelican Ventures, LLC

Publishing History
First White Rose Edition, 2016
Paperback Edition ISBN 978-1-61116-984-3
Electronic Edition ISBN 978-1-61116-985-0
Published in the United States of America

Dedication

To the amazing ladies at the Seekerville Blog. Your encouragement and support helped make my dream come true. Thanks to you all!

Other Books in the Rainbow Falls Series

Betrayed Hearts
Wayward Hearts

1

Chloe Martin blamed it on the rain.

Her bus from New York had been delayed, and once she arrived in her hometown of Rainbow Falls, North Dakota, their sole taxi cab was otherwise engaged, leaving her to walk into town in her waterlogged stilettos, creating new blisters at every step.

She almost wept with relief when she reached McIntyre Street, and the familiar two-story house came into view. The glow of an exterior light illuminated her cousin's rental property. Chloe lugged her suitcases up and paused under the porch roof to swipe water out of her eyes. She took a moment to let her breathing even out and to survey her surroundings. From what she could see, the place hadn't changed much.

Her cousin, Nick, had bought the residence several years ago and renovated it, turning the house into two separate living quarters. Nick now worked as a minister at the community church, but he continued to rent out the apartments. His upstairs tenant had recently moved out, providing Chloe with a temporary, rent-free haven until she could figure out what to do with her now imploded life.

A sharp sting of grief surfaced. If only her mother were still alive, waiting for her. But Mama was gone, and Chloe's childhood home now belonged to a nice couple with a young son and a golden retriever. At least Mama wasn't around to learn of her daughter's shame.

Chloe turned her focus to the problem at hand. She would need a key to get in. Nick usually kept one under the flowerpot beside the front door; however, she found it stuck in the soggy soil among the still blooming geraniums. She pulled it out and brushed away the dirt.

The crisp autumn breeze chilled her as she struggled to fit the grimy key into the lock. No matter how hard she jiggled, her cold-stiffened fingers could not seem to budge it.

Shivering, Chloe peered through the side window, trying to recall what Nick had told her about the current tenant on the main floor. Would he or she be awake at this late hour? All Chloe wanted was a hot shower, dry clothes, and a soft bed. With no choice but to disturb her new neighbor, she rapped the brass knocker.

"Hello. Is anyone home?" When no one responded, she tried again. "Anyone? Please!"

Maybe he had the TV on or was wearing headphones.

She searched for a doorbell, found one, and jabbed the button. No answer.

Leaning her forehead against the door, she tried to gather the mental fortitude to determine her next course of action. She couldn't use her cellphone to call Nick because the battery had died hours ago. Maybe she'd walk around the back.

Without warning, the door flew inward.

Chloe shrieked, teetered, and then fell right into something firm and warm. The air whooshed out of her lungs.

"Whoa. Steady there." Strong hands grasped her

elbows, supporting her.

"I—I'm sorry." She fisted a hand in his shirt until the world righted. She managed to take a step back and peered through wet strands of hair at the dark-haired man. Strong cheekbones, full lips and a cleft chin made quite an appealing picture—if she'd been in a mood to notice.

"Are you all right?"

"I think so." She frowned at the damp splotches on his chest.

He pointed to the key in the doorknob. "Looks like your key isn't working. Sure you have the right address?"

She attempted to appear confident and trustworthy—a difficult feat when she likely looked like a drowned cat. "Yes. My cousin, Nick Logan, owns this place. He's letting me stay here for a while."

The man's eyebrows shot upward. "Chloe Martin?" Disbelief rang in his voice.

"That's right," she said cautiously. "And who are you?"

~*~

Aidan North scrubbed a hand over his jaw. How could this possibly be Nick's little cousin? The last time he'd seen Chloe Martin—close to ten years ago now—she'd been a scrawny teenager with a mouthful of braces, hanging out with his younger sister, Maxi. This woman was no teenager. And definitely not scrawny.

She'd turned into one gorgeous woman. Ropes of dark hair hung over her shoulders. Large brown eyes stared at him, marred only by the slight frown between her thin eyebrows.

"I'm Aidan North," he said. "Maxi's brother."

"Aidan?" She squinted at him in the dim hallway. "I thought you lived in Arizona."

"I did for a while. I'm back home now."

Her eyes widened. "*You're* Nick's main floor tenant?"

"That's right."

"I guess Nick didn't tell you he's letting me use the upstairs apartment. Unfortunately, the spare key he left wouldn't work."

Aidan frowned. Why hadn't Nick told him to expect Chloe tonight? He pulled the key out of the lock. "Maybe if it wasn't covered in mud…" Aidan lifted his gaze to a saturated Chloe. *Geesh*. He did *not* need this problem tonight. The paperwork for his new youth center was due tomorrow.

A tremor ran through Chloe's frame, and her teeth chattered.

Aidan's chivalrous instincts kicked in. *So much for paperwork*. "Come on. You need to get dry." He lugged her two enormous suitcases inside and closed the door. "Let me get you a towel and a hot drink."

"Th-Thank you, but no. I just want to go upstairs." Exhaustion lined her features.

"OK. I'll carry your bags."

"Thank you."

Aidan grabbed the soggy cases–that weighed slightly less than a small pickup–and followed Chloe up the narrow staircase. Droplets fell from her jacket, leaving tiny puddles. How on earth did she walk in those shoes? No wonder she was limping.

She stopped on the upper landing. "You don't have a key for this door, do you?"

He set one suitcase down and pulled the key from

his pocket. He wiped it off and attempted to slide by her. "Sorry. Just let me reach around…"

His hand brushed her arm. The spike in his pulse made his fingers clumsy. When the door creaked open, the musty smell of an unused room wafted out. He turned on the lights and deposited the bags inside.

"You'll have to air the place out. Nick hasn't had a tenant for a few weeks." He flicked more lights on and found the bathroom, glad to discover it was supplied with essentials. He grabbed a towel off the hook and returned to the living room. "Here. You should probably get into something dry."

"Thanks." Shivering, she took the towel and grabbed one of her cases.

The scent of wet clothes and fruity shampoo drifted by him.

Aidan let out a slow breath. Tension remained coiled in every muscle, giving him the distinct impression that his life had just taken an unexpected—and unwelcome—twist.

~*~

Chloe closed the bedroom door and leaned against it with an inward groan.

Aidan North. The guy she'd both adored and loathed, as only a teenage girl could do. Her cheeks heated at the memories. She'd always dropped things or knocked into furniture around him. Tonight, she hadn't recognized him—though something about him had seemed familiar. The voice, deeper now, could still send a thrill through her.

And she'd made a fool of herself—again!

Chloe unzipped one of the suitcases and rifled

through the damp clothes for some dry jeans and a sweatshirt. She longed for a hot shower, but it could wait. A sigh of relief escaped as she slipped off her heels and sank her toes into the throw rug by the bed. She changed, hung her wet things in the bathroom, and grabbed a towel for her hair.

Maybe Aidan would be gone. But she found him standing at the counter in the galley kitchen, kettle in hand. A crop of dark, wavy hair skimmed his high forehead, highlighting a straight nose and strong jaw line. His toned physique and muscled forearms were very different from the thin, wiry frame she remembered. Maxi's bookish brother had turned into a hunk.

"What are you doing?"

He looked up. "Making you a cup of tea. The last tenant left some teabags in the cupboard. Hope you don't mind it black."

She looped the towel around her neck and accepted the cup, trying to be gracious. "Thanks. You didn't have to do this."

"Are you kidding? Nick would have my hide if I didn't help. Maxi too."

Chloe smiled. "Wouldn't want to engage the wrath of Maxi. How is she, by the way? We haven't talked much since the baby arrived." *Safe topic. Keep it neutral.*

His eyes softened. "Never better. Little Ben is the light of her life."

Envy took hold of Chloe's heart, but she smothered it. No use wishing for something she didn't deserve. "I'm glad Maxi's happy." She sipped the tea, relishing the warmth. "I don't mean to be rude, but if I don't sit down, my feet will explode." She hoped he'd take the hint and leave.

Instead he followed her into the cozy living room.

She scanned the taupe walls, mahogany fireplace, and comfy furniture. Nothing had changed since her sister had lived here five years earlier. Chloe sank into the overstuffed green sofa and raised her feet onto the plush cushions with a sigh. She might never budge again.

Aidan snapped on two brass lamps, giving the room a warm glow. His eyes narrowed as he crouched and raised her foot. "You've got a bunch of blisters. How far did you walk?"

She snatched her foot away, her pulse zigzagging. "From the bus stop."

"You walked all that way in those ridiculous shoes?"

She stiffened at his tone. "They're not ridiculous. And unlike New York, there aren't cabs waiting at every corner."

"Why didn't you call Nick?"

"Because he's got two toddlers and a pregnant wife at home. He didn't need to rescue me."

Aidan muttered something about stubborn women and disappeared down the hallway. The clatter of cupboard doors opening and closing sounded. A few seconds later, he reappeared with a box of bandages and a cloth. He sat down in front of her and lifted one of her feet onto his lap.

"What do you think you're doing?" She attempted to pull free, but he tightened his grip.

"I'm a vice-principal, remember? I'm used to dealing with stubborn adolescents."

Annoyed, she crossed her arms. "I'm not an adolescent, in case you haven't noticed."

He looked up from his ministrations. "Oh, I've noticed, believe me."

A streak of heat rushed to her cheeks. The perfect scathing reply escaped her frazzled brain.

As he began to work on her feet, any objection she had melted away. With the last bandage in place, he patted her foot, and set it back on the couch.

She let out a contented sigh. It had been a long time since anyone had taken care of her. "Thank you. That feels much better."

"You're welcome." He settled into the couch and flung his arm over the back. "So what brings you home? I thought you had a great job in some swanky New York restaurant."

Tension seeped back into her body. "I'm here to help Nick and Lily until they can hire a nanny."

"You're not here for long then?"

Did he sound disappointed or relieved?

She gave a non-committal shrug. "We'll have to see how it goes."

Before he could interrogate her further, she countered with questions of her own. "What about you? Last I heard, you were teaching in Arizona."

Wariness flickered in his gray eyes, but his voice remained even. "There was an opening at Rainbow High for vice-principal. I applied and got the job."

"That's quite the career advancement for someone your age." A grudging respect wormed its way through her resentment.

"It helped that the principal has known me a long time." He gave a lop-sided grin. "Mr. Jenkins was my math teacher in twelfth grade. If anyone told me he'd be my boss one day, I never would have believed it."

"I'll bet." The warmth of the tea and the easing of

the pain in her feet allowed Chloe to relax. A yawn escaped before she could hide it.

"I should let you get some rest." Aidan rose. "If you need a ride to Nick's tomorrow, I can run you over. I leave for work around seven thirty." He studied her, an unreadable expression on his face. "It's good to have you back, Chloe."

She attempted to rise, but he held up a hand.

"No need to get up. I'll see myself out." The glow of the lamp created a halo effect around his head.

"OK. Thanks…for everything."

"My pleasure." A teasing smile created a dimple in one cheek. "It's not every day I get bowled over by a beautiful woman." He winked and disappeared out the door.

Chloe sat open-mouthed trying to wrap her head around the fact that Aidan North thought she was beautiful.

2

Though she would have loved to laze in bed, Chloe rose early the next morning, knowing her sister needed her. She showered and dressed, then fastened her treasured gold locket around her neck—the one Lily had given her when she'd left for college.

Her sister had come into her life after the two of them had grown up in different adoptive families. When Lily arrived in Rainbow Falls looking for Chloe, Lily had met and fallen in love with Nick. Nick took one look at Lily and he'd been a goner.

Chloe caressed the filigree etching in the locket. Inside, a small black and white photo of their biological mother held a place of honor. On the other side, Chloe had added a picture of her adoptive mother, Sonia Martin, who'd passed away two years earlier. Chloe liked to envision both of her mothers watching over her from heaven. She closed the lid with a soft click. What would these good women think of the mess she'd made of her life?

Chloe brushed her hair and twisted it into a tidy ponytail. The sight of the ugly burn mark on her left arm made her grimace–a souvenir from her last night at the restaurant.

No point in dwelling on the past. She needed a new plan for her life. Her original dream of opening a bakery—a dream sidetracked by her ill-fated romance—still hovered in her mind. Perhaps there was a way to make it a reality. Maybe even here in Rainbow Falls.

But all that would have to wait until Lily's situation improved. Nick and Lily were the only family she had left. Chloe could put her own plans on hold until they no longer needed her.

As much as she hated to deal with Aidan North again, her battered feet couldn't take the walk to Lily's. She grabbed her purse and jacket and headed down to his main-floor apartment.

Aidan answered her knock right away, looking very professional in a dark gray suit, crisp white shirt, and silver tie. Chloe didn't remember vice-principals ever looking *this* good.

She gave a bright smile. "I'm here to take you up on your offer of a ride—if it's still OK."

"Sure. Come in. I'm almost ready." He took a swig from a mug and waved her in.

The aroma of coffee filled his apartment, making Chloe's mouth water. Where was a good café when you needed one?

"Help yourself to some coffee," Aidan said and vanished down the hall.

In his surprisingly tidy kitchen, she found a mug, poured the coffee, and added cream. She wandered out to admire the living room with its large stone fireplace and built-in bookcases. His personal touches—a few magazines, his laptop on the table, the trendy artwork on the walls—gave the room a cozy, lived-in feel.

"Ready?" Aidan reappeared with a briefcase in hand.

"Sure. Just let me rinse this cup." Several minutes later, buckled into Aidan's sports car, Chloe stole a glance at him.

He drove with quiet confidence, his eyes shaded by mirrored sunglasses. As if sensing her gaze, he turned toward her. "It's nice what you're doing to help your sister. How long do you think it'll take to find a suitable nanny?"

"Hopefully not long."

"What about your job? Are you taking vacation time?" Aidan pushed his glasses up on his head. Sunlight gleamed off his perfectly groomed dark hair and flecks of gold flashed in his gray eyes.

"Something like that." She wasn't ready to talk about her job or the real reason she'd come home.

Aidan turned into Nick's driveway and shifted into park.

"Uh, thanks for the ride. I appreciate it." Chloe jumped out, in case he was about to question her further. When she reached the porch steps and looked back, Aidan was still in the driveway.

She'd avoided his curiosity; however, she doubted Lily and Nick would let the matter go as easily.

~*~

Chloe walked in without knocking and followed the voices to the kitchen.

Nick juggled one girl on his shoulder and the other on his hip, his blond hair standing up in messy tufts. An upended box of cereal lay on the kitchen table with a trail spilled across the floor. "Chloe." The relief in his voice would have been comical if not for the lines of exhaustion around his eyes. "Thank goodness you're here."

A surge of love crashed over her. How she'd missed this man—her champion, her defender, her surrogate older brother. "Hey, cuz. You look like you could use some help." She kissed his cheek and plucked her younger niece, Laura, off his shoulder. "Hi, sweetheart. I'm your Aunt Chloe."

The one-year-old stared at her with big, blue eyes.

Three-year-old Annabelle, however, bounced on her father's hip. "Auntie Chlo."

"Hello, Miss Annabelle." Chloe smacked a loud kiss on her cheek. "Are you being a good girl?"

Annabelle twirled a dark curl around one finger and nodded.

"Of course you are. Why don't you help Daddy sweep up the cereal while I say hi to your mommy?"

"Mommy's sick." The large brown eyes went wide.

"I know, but she'll get better soon. And then you'll have a new baby in the family."

"Don't want a baby." Her perfect little lips pouted.

"The B-word is a no-no around here." Nick chuckled.

"I see." Chloe hid a grin as she plopped Laura into the high chair and handed her a sippy cup. "After I come down, we'll play with your toys."

"And Daddy can get some work done." Nick set Annabelle on the floor and opened the broom closet. "Lily's not in the best of moods. Having you here should perk her up."

"Let's hope so." But as Chloe mounted the staircase, the thought of telling her sister about her ordeal in New York made the coffee curdle in her stomach. With Lily and the unborn baby's health in the balance, Chloe could not dump her problems on her sister.

As for Nick... Her heart stilled. How could she

confess her transgressions to her devout cousin, minister of the town's most popular church? Could he ever forgive her?

Could God?

She paused outside the master bedroom and took a deep breath before knocking on the door.

"Come in." The grumpy voice did not match the invitation.

Chloe forced her lips into a smile and opened the door.

Lily sat propped against pillows, her belly a curved mound under the quilt. Her dark hair, so similar to Chloe's, poofed out around her.

"Hey, sis. How are you feeling?" Chloe's heart swelled.

A huge smile transformed Lily's face from grumpy to radiant. "Chloe. You're home."

"Yes, I am." Chloe gathered her into a warm hug.

Lily held her tight and when she finally released her, tears leaked from her brown eyes.

Alarm raced through Chloe. Lily wasn't supposed to be upset. "Hey, it can't be that bad."

"You try being confined to bed with two girls who need their mommy."

Chloe grabbed a tissue from a box on the nightstand and plopped down beside Lily. "It must be frustrating."

"It is." Lily sniffed and took the tissue. "Annabelle doesn't understand why Mommy won't do things with her anymore. It breaks my heart to disappoint her."

"I'm sure the doctor wouldn't confine you to bed if it wasn't necessary. What exactly is the problem?"

"My blood pressure has gone crazy. Doc's worried about a stroke."

A stroke? Chloe's hand stilled. "Well, then you need to focus on your health and that baby's. Better to miss a couple of months now, than to miss their whole lives."

"I know." Lily blew her nose. "But I can't help going stir crazy. And the hormones are making me cranky."

Chloe looked around. Heavy drapes darkened the dreary room.

"No wonder you're feeling gloomy. Let's get some light in here." She threw back the curtains, and sunshine streamed in, immediately brightening the space. "That's better. Maybe we can set you up on the couch downstairs for a while this afternoon. Give you a change of scenery."

Through her tears, Lily managed a smile. "I'm so glad you're here. How did you get time off work?"

Chloe straightened the covers, not meeting Lily's gaze. "Paul understands that family issues come up." That part was true. Paul Decourcy, her boss and owner of *Oliver's Emporium*, believed in the importance of family.

"And what about Richard?"

There it was—the same stabbing pain every time someone mentioned his name. She exhaled slowly. "Richard and I broke up."

"Oh, honey. I'm so sorry. What happened?"

Chloe shivered, remembering their last encounter. Wounds too fresh and raw choked her. "I can't talk about it yet. I'm sorry..."

"Sure. I understand."

But the hurt expression on Lily's face filled Chloe with guilt.

How could she ever tell her sister the truth?

~*~

Aidan shut down the computer in his office. Chloe's nervous reaction to his questions this morning had puzzled him all day. Her haunted look hinted at some type of trauma. Had she come back for another reason besides helping Lily?

Annoyed at himself, Aidan picked up his briefcase. Chloe's life was none of his concern. The fact that a very attractive woman had moved in upstairs need not change his routine. In fact, they'd probably never see each other. Just as well. A woman was a complication he did not need. Or want.

He locked his office and walked out to his car. Instead of heading home, he pulled onto the gravel road leading to Maxi and Jason's farmhouse on the outskirts of town. The bright flag over the fire station, built on the property Jason had donated to the town, flapped in the wind.

Every time he drove in here, memories of growing up on the farm, of his father trying to pressure Aidan and his siblings to take over the family business, flooded him. When his dad passed away several years ago, his mother had been forced to sell the property due to ill health, and Jason Hanley had purchased the land. Little did they know that Maxi would end up marrying Jason and living back on the family homestead.

The screen door opened and Maxi emerged, her auburn hair pulled back in a stubby ponytail. She carried one-year-old Ben on her hip. "Hey, Aidan. What are you doing here?" Surprise and pleasure lit her features.

"Nice to see you too, sis." He climbed the stairs, gave her kiss, and took the squirming toddler from her arms. "How's my favorite nephew?"

The child gurgled in response and grabbed a handful of Aidan's hair.

"Come on in. I'm cooking dinner. Jason should be home soon."

He sat with Ben on his knee at the big wooden table, one of the original furnishings Maxi had kept.

She stirred a pan on the stove. "We haven't seen much of you lately. How are things at school?"

"The usual. Chaos for a few weeks until things settle into a routine. What's new with you?"

"Not much. Ben's cutting another molar, so he's been a bit cranky." She shot a glance at him as she put the lid on the pan. "I took Mama into Kingsville last week to see the specialist."

A bolt of shame slammed through Aidan. He'd forgotten all about his mother's appointment to check on her multiple sclerosis and had neglected to follow up. "Sorry, Max. The date totally slipped my mind. What did the doctors say?"

"They were very pleased with Mama. She's still in remission, and in fact, they feel she's improved somewhat."

"That's great news. Working with you and Peg at the hair salon seems to have given her a new lease on life."

"Who knew she and Jason's mom would become best friends and roomies." She shook her head. "Jason and I tried to convince her to move back here, but she loves living with Peg. They get along so well, and Peg spoils Mama."

"Now that Peg doesn't have Jason to coddle, she

needs someone to look after. I'll give Mom a call tonight."

"Good. She'd like that." Maxi pulled a pitcher of iced tea from the fridge. "So, how's the youth center project coming along?"

"I think I've got a building lined up, but I need more volunteers before I can go any further." The teens needed somewhere to hang out to keep them out of trouble—a mission Aidan vowed to make a reality.

"Well, it's a great idea and I'm sure you'll win people over." She grabbed two glasses from the cupboard.

"I hope so."

Ben squealed with delight as Aiden bounced him on his knee.

Maxi set the jug on the table. "Not that I'm complaining, but what brings you by?"

"Do I need a reason?"

"No, but you look as if you've got something on your mind."

He gave a half-shrug. "Guess who landed—quite literally—on my doorstep last night?"

"Who?"

"Chloe Martin."

"Chloe's home?" A grin stretched across Maxi's face, brightening her hazel eyes. "I didn't think she'd be able to get away from her job."

"I asked her if she's taking vacation time, and she got real jumpy. Any idea what's going on with her?"

Maxi speared him with a shrewd look. "Since when are you so interested in Chloe? Seems to me you couldn't stand her years ago. Or was it Chloe who couldn't stand you?"

Aidan ignored the question. "Anyway, she's living

above me. I just thought you'd want to know she's home." He should've known Maxi would read something into his innocent queries. He jerked to his feet and handed Ben to her. "Sorry, just remembered something I have to take care of. Say hi to Jason for me."

And before his sister could jump to any crazy conclusions about his interest in Chloe Martin, Aidan escaped out the front door.

3

Chloe slumped onto the couch, too tired to even turn on the TV. Who knew minding two toddlers could be so exhausting? A busy Saturday night at *Oliver's* seemed far easier to manage than motherhood.

At least it kept her from obsessing about her train-wreck of a life. Chloe's eyes drifted closed until her cellphone rang. Groaning, she fished it out of her pocket.

"Just when are you planning to come by? I had to hear from Aidan that you're in town."

"Maxi. Hi." A wave of guilt swept over her. "I've been meaning to call, but watching those two munchkins is taking every ounce of energy."

The laughter on the other end made Chloe feel better. Maxi would never hold a grudge.

"I know how busy kids can keep you. How's Lily?"

"Going stir crazy. But her blood pressure's down, so the bed rest is working."

"I'm glad. Hey, can you come for dinner tomorrow? I'm dying for you to meet the new love of my life."

Chloe chuckled at Maxi's smitten tone. "I'd love to. Nick's usually home by five."

"See you around six then?"

"Sure. Can I bring anything?"

"Just your adorable self. See you tomorrow."

Chloe tossed the phone onto the coffee table and lay back. A hot bath sounded like heaven. If only she had a maid to fill the tub. She stayed there, hovering in the delicious state between sleep and wakefulness, until a loud clap of thunder shook the room, jolting Chloe back to full consciousness. Shivering, she reached over to turn on a lamp. When had it started to storm?

The lights flickered for a second, and Chloe shot to her feet. A cold sweat broke out over her whole body. *Please don't let the power go out.*

She'd always been terrified of the dark, a fear that magnified during thunderstorms. And lately she'd been experiencing an escalation in anxiety attacks. Richard used to help her manage the symptoms, holding her until she calmed down. Now she was on her own.

"Nick must keep candles around here somewhere." It helped to talk out loud, as though someone else was in the apartment.

She yanked out every drawer and searched the cupboards. Not a candle, not a match. Not even a flashlight. Maybe she should go to bed. That way if the power went out, she'd be asleep and wouldn't even notice.

Another clap of thunder exploded.

Chloe shrieked. Before she could reach her cellphone, the lights flickered again. She held her breath. *Stay on, stay on. Please stay on.*

Everything went black and an incredible stillness descended. The whir of electronics ceased, leaving her in deathly silence.

Chloe stood rigid, perspiration snaking down her back. The light from her phone became her beacon of hope. She pounced, clutching it to her chest, and took deep, even breaths to ward off the anxiety. Why couldn't she conquer her fear? Her baby nieces were probably braver than this.

She punched in Nick's number, but after two rings, she disconnected. He had his hands full with Lily and the girls. If he heard the panic in her voice, he'd feel obliged to come over.

No, she'd handle this on her own—somehow.

Chloe couldn't dispel her rising apprehension. She had to get some light, or she'd have a full-blown meltdown. Maybe Aidan had some spare candles.

The glow from her phone did little to penetrate the inkiness of the staircase. She slid her foot out until she came to the first step. Holding tight to the railing, she inched her way down, one stair at a time. Only her labored breathing broke the eerie silence.

The hallway below seemed even darker. She was nearing the bottom, when something furry brushed by her bare foot. She screamed and flailed both hands. Her phone launched into the air as she landed on the floor with a crash. White-hot fire shot through her shoulder and hip.

Seconds later, the clatter of footsteps registered through the haze of pain.

"Chloe, is that you?" Aidan's deep voice echoed in the space.

"Aidan." Relief spilled through her. "I'm by the stairs."

His flickering candle cast grotesque shadows on the walls.

"What happened? You didn't fall all the way down, did you?"

"Just the last step or two. Can you help me up?"

"Not yet." He set the holder on the ground. "We need to make sure nothing's broken."

The grip of fear eased. She wasn't alone, and the small flame broke the overpowering darkness.

Warm hands moved swiftly over her legs and arms. Somehow in the dark, the process seemed incredibly intimate. He moved to her head and neck, but when he touched her right shoulder, searing heat forced a gasp from her throat.

"Sorry. Bear with me a minute more." He finished his assessment, and then before she could protest, lifted her into his arms.

When he stepped away from the candle, she immediately stiffened.

"Am I hurting you?"

"No." She closed her eyes to pretend the darkness didn't exist and lowered her head to his shoulder. When she opened her eyes, she found they had entered his apartment. Several candles burned on various tables, bathing the room in a soothing glow.

Aidan placed her on the couch. "I'll be back in a minute." He reappeared soon after with the candle and her phone. "Why were you on the stairs in the dark?"

"I was coming to see if you had any spare candles. Then something furry ran over my foot on the way down." She shuddered. "I think it was a big rat."

Aidan laughed out loud.

She bristled. "I don't see how this is funny."

"It wasn't a rat," he said. "It was my cat, Leo. He gets crazy when there's a storm. I was trying to get him to come inside, but he bolted upstairs instead."

"Oh." She was relieved to know the building wasn't infested with rodents.

"I'm sorry if Leo caused your fall. Let me get you

some ice." He returned with an ice pack, placed it on her shoulder, and then sat down beside her. "You sure you're not hurt anywhere else?"

The spicy scent of his aftershave filled her senses. "I'll be fine. I'm always hurting something. Truth is I'm a bit of a klutz."

His gaze met hers. "So how does a klutz become a chef without losing fingers?" He lifted one of her hands in an exaggerated examination.

The warmth of his fingers sent tingles of awareness up her arm. She pulled her hand away in the pretense of securing the ice pack. "I'm not clumsy in the kitchen. Never lost a vegetable."

He grinned. The flicker from one of the candles reflected in his eyes, almost hypnotizing her.

She lowered her gaze. The intimate setting suddenly seemed far too romantic. She needed to put some distance between her and the compelling Aidan North. "If I could borrow a candle or a flashlight, I'll let you get back to whatever you were doing."

He smiled. "You do have a way of crashing in on me."

Thunder boomed again.

Chloe yelped and clutched Aidan's arm. The ice pack slipped off her shoulder and disappeared into the cushions of the couch. "Sorry. I have a thing about storms…and the dark."

Aidan didn't make fun of her fears. Instead he covered her hand. "Then you'll get along fine with Leo. Although he doesn't seem to mind the dark." He pulled her wrist up.

For a split second, she thought he intended to kiss her hand.

He frowned. "What happened here?"

"Nothing. Cooks get burns all the time."

"I thought you said you weren't clumsy in the kitchen."

"I'm not." *Only when someone shoves me into a hot stove.* She jerked to her feet, tugging her sleeves down. "Could I have that candle now, please?"

~*~

Aidan rose. If he weren't so used to dealing with fibbing teens, he wouldn't have known she was lying. But why would she lie about a burn? "What really happened, Chloe?"

Her chin quivered. "Nothing I want to talk about."

Had someone hurt her? His protective instincts roared to life.

"Talking about a problem usually helps. The incident loses its power once it's out in the open."

"Sounds like you're speaking from experience."

"Let's just say I didn't leave my old job on the best of terms."

"Why? What happened?"

He shoved his hands into his pant pockets. "Long story."

"Tell you what. When you're ready to spill your secrets, I'll spill mine."

She had him there. Why should she bare her soul to him when he wasn't willing to do the same? "Message received. I'll mind my own business."

With the candlelight dancing over her, she looked like a fairy tale princess—a lovely damsel in distress. That was exactly how his problems started in Arizona, trying to help a student in trouble.

A flash of lightning illuminated the room.

He needed to stay far, far away from women needing rescue. Especially beautiful ones who dulled his senses. He handed her a candle. "Here. Take this. I'll get you a couple of spares in case this one burns down." He strode into the kitchen, pulled out a box of utility candles and a pack of matches. "There you go. These should last for a few storms."

"Thanks for your help."

"You're welcome." He avoided looking into those mesmerizing eyes, picked up another candleholder, and motioned to the door. "Come on. I'll walk you up."

4

Despite the blisters on her feet and a stiff hip, Chloe walked up the main street of Rainbow Falls the next afternoon, enjoying an ice cream.

Nick's afternoon appointment at the church had ended sooner than anticipated, and he'd come home early with good news. He'd found a nanny for the girls.

Chloe had to admit she'd be glad for more time to focus on her plans for the future.

She inhaled the crisp, clean air. A sense of rightness, of homecoming, filled her with well-being. When she'd left for college, she'd been eager to leave Rainbow Falls behind, but her hometown held a great deal more appeal than she remembered.

She'd given considerable thought to what she wanted to do now. She was tired of working for someone else and not being in charge of her own career. Maybe being fired from *Oliver's* had been a blessing in disguise, a chance to start the business she'd always dreamed of.

She let her mind wander to the idea she'd kept tucked away for years. While attending culinary school in New York, she'd devised a business plan for a bakery and coffee shop, but had never had the courage to act on it. Instead, she'd worked for Paul, gaining the experience—and the confidence—to one day branch out on her own. Would that type of establishment work in Rainbow Falls? Goose bumps erupted at the prospect.

She crossed the street, seeing her town through new eyes. The police station, the library, Peg's Cut N Curl, and of course, Ruby's Diner. Her favorite local eatery might pose the main source of competition for the business she envisioned.

A block down from Peg's, Chloe spotted a For Lease sign in a storefront window. She frowned, trying to recall what had been there before. She cupped a hand and peered through the grimy window. Small round tables and wicker chairs sat pushed against the far right wall. On the left, a counter and cash register remained. The menu board indicated the place had been a sandwich shop. A tingle of excitement raced up her spine. This was exactly the type of setting she'd pictured.

She jotted down the real estate number and looked at her watch. She needed to go home and change for dinner at Maxi's. If she hurried, she might have enough time to call the agent. Back at the house, she checked the mailbox out of habit, and then opened the front door.

A big, orange tabby sat on the mat inside, regarding her with a faintly bored expression.

"You must be Leo. I should be mad at you, but since you share my fear of storms, I'll let it go."

Leo stretched and curled around her ankles.

Chloe laughed. "I think we'll get along just fine, Leo." She stepped over him and climbed the stairs. With time to spare after changing, she pulled out the realtor's phone number and placed the call.

"Myra Goodwin, Royal Realty."

"Ms. Goodwin, my name is Chloe Martin. I'm

calling about the shop for lease on McIntyre Street."

"An excellent choice. Good location. Reasonable rent. What did you have in mind for the place?"

"A bakery and coffee shop." Saying it out loud made her hand tremble.

"Hmm. A bakery just might work in that space."

"I'd like to take a better look at the interior, if possible."

"Of course. How does Monday morning around nine o'clock sound?"

"Perfect." She made a mental note to let Nick know.

"Great. I'll meet you there."

Chloe ended the call and did a little happy dance. She'd taken the first step toward creating a new life, a life far removed from Richard Highmore and the drama at *Oliver's*. For the first time in weeks, a flicker of hope shimmered within her reach.

Still riding a wave of euphoria half an hour later, Chloe drove Lily's car into Maxi and Jason's driveway.

At the sight of Maxi's farmhouse, memories arose of sitting on her friend's veranda in the summer, of them sipping lemonade surrounded by the scent of freshly cut hay, which Maxi hated, but Chloe secretly loved. A hot rush of nostalgia tightened Chloe's throat.

Maxi welcomed her with a fierce hug. "It's great to see you, Chlo. I wish New York wasn't so far away."

"I know. I miss you too." Chloe swallowed and stepped back with the sudden, sharp awareness of the huge hole in her life. She'd missed Maxi and Lily more than she realized. Missed their girl chats and sharing ice cream sundaes at Ruby's. No wonder she'd fallen so quickly for Richard's charms.

The spiky red hair of Maxi's youth had been

tamed into a smooth, chin-length bob. Her eyes glowed with happiness.

"You look great. Motherhood definitely agrees with you."

"Except for these five extra pounds I can't seem to lose. But Jason doesn't mind. Says I was too skinny before." Maxi grinned and patted her stomach.

"So where's this little man who has you wrapped around his finger?"

Love beamed from Maxi's hazel eyes. "He's napping right now. Should be awake any minute. In the meantime, come keep me company while I cook." She hooked her arm through Chloe's and pulled her to the kitchen. "So, how is good old New York these days?"

"Cutthroat as usual."

"Good to know, in case I ever get a yearning to go back."

"And leave Peg's? You'd be crazy." Chloe chuckled.

Maxi had left the infamous *Baronne's Salon* to marry Jason and work at his mother's beauty shop, a decision she clearly didn't regret. Maxi pulled an apron from the back of a chair and secured it around her waist.

Chloe almost laughed at the picture of domesticity her friend exuded. A far cry from the *fashionista* who'd left Rainbow Falls for the lure of the big city.

A heap of vegetables lay in disarray on the long kitchen counter.

Chloe itched to grab a cleaver. "You need some help in here?"

"I was hoping you'd offer. I'm making a salad to go with the chili and biscuits."

"Consider it done." Chloe chose the biggest knife from the drawer, found a wooden board, and began to chop.

"I spoke to Lily yesterday." Maxi stirred a big pot on the stove. "She's very happy to have you home."

Her casual tone didn't fool Chloe for a minute.

"I'm glad I can help."

"She's worried about you though."

"She is?" Chloe stiffened, anticipating an unpleasant twist to the conversation.

"She told me you broke up with Richard."

Chloe's hand stilled on the knife. "That's right."

"Well, are you going to tell me what happened? Or do I have to torture the answer out of you?" Maxi banged the lid back on the pot.

Chloe put the knife down and wiped her hands on a towel. Confession was supposed to be good for the soul, and if anyone's soul needed help, hers did. "You have to promise not to tell Nick or Lily."

Maxi pushed a strand of auburn hair behind one ear and frowned. "I don't know if I can do that."

"Fair enough." Chloe continued chopping carrots into tiny bits.

Maxi came up beside her at the counter. "Can you at least tell me what happened at work? Lily gets the impression you might be out of a job."

Chloe blinked. How had Lily picked up on that? "She's right. I got fired."

Maxi gasped. "What? Why would they fire their best chef?"

Chloe shrugged. "Fallout from the break up. Richard is co-owner of *Oliver's* and Paul Decourcy is his best friend."

"What does that have to do with anything?"

"Richard put pressure on Paul to get rid of me. Paul didn't want to, but what could he do with Richard threatening to pull his capital out of the restaurant?"

Maxi banged a wooden spoon on the chopping block. "What a jerk." She turned to fix Chloe with a thoughtful look. "If Richard was that angry, I take it *you* broke up with *him*."

Chloe's back stiffened at the barrage of horrible memories. The ugly words hurled in anger. "I did."

"What happened?"

Chloe kept her eyes on the tomato as she sliced it neatly in half. "The relationship wasn't working out."

"Did he cheat on you?"

The word *cheat* reverberated in her chest.

Maxi's relentless gaze bored into her.

How could Chloe possibly answer that question without losing her best friend's respect?

"Hope I'm not late." Aidan's booming voice accompanied the creak of the screen door.

Chloe exhaled. *Saved, for the moment.*

~*~

Aidan's brain took a moment to register the fact that Chloe Martin was standing in his sister's kitchen, dicing vegetables. He gave an inward groan. His plan for a nice, relaxing dinner with Maxi and Jason evaporated faster than the steam rising from the pots on the stove. Now he'd have to guard his reaction to the tempting woman.

"Hey, Aidan." Maxi bounced over to kiss his cheek. "You know Chloe, right? Your new neighbor."

He threw a pointed look at his sister. "I didn't

realize this was a dinner party."

"What party? I haven't seen Chloe yet, and I wanted her to meet Ben."

As if on cue, wails emerged from the baby monitor on the table. "Speaking of which, excuse me while I go change his diaper. Be right back." With a wicked gleam in her eye, Maxi patted Aidan's arm on the way out.

Chloe had returned to her chopping. Her long mane of hair shrouded her face as she worked. Every few seconds, she pushed the hair back with her forearm. Why did he find that tiny gesture so irresistible? He opened the fridge and took out a pitcher of lemonade. "You want a drink?" He hoped his voice sounded normal, not churning with the emotions he was trying to tamp down.

"Sure."

He poured two glasses and handed her one.

"Thanks." She stopped working to take it, darting a quick smile in his direction.

"No problem. How's the shoulder today?"

"A little stiff, but no lasting damage." She took a long drink. "Oh, I met Leo this afternoon. He was standing guard in the hallway."

"I hope he behaved himself. He doesn't take well to strangers."

"He was friendly with me. Purred around my ankles, in fact."

"Huh. He's never done that before."

"Must be our shared dread of thunderstorms." She grinned.

"Here we are, all cleaned up." Maxi strode into the room with little Ben in her arms.

The toddler, still not totally awake, pressed his face into his mother's neck.

"Chloe, this is Benjamin Charles Hanley. Ben, this is Mommy's good friend, Chloe."

"Hi, Ben." Chloe gave the child such a blinding smile that Aidan forgot to breathe. Then she reached over and ran a finger down the boy's cheek. "He's adorable, Maxi." The awe in her voice caused goose bumps to ripple across Aidan's neck.

"I know. I thank God every day for such a wonderful gift." Maxi pushed the curls off Ben's forehead. "How about a snack, buddy?"

Ben nodded.

"Here, Uncle Aidan. Put him in his chair, please." Maxi's request tore Aidan's attention from Chloe.

Aidan took the toddler and tossed him in the air. High-pitched giggles erupted. He swung the boy into the high chair and clipped the belt around him before Ben knew what had happened.

The front door banged open again.

A cheerful whistle announced the arrival of his brother-in-law, Jason.

"How's my favorite family?" The broad-shouldered man strode into the kitchen and stopped with a look of surprise. "Wow. Full house tonight. Hi, Aidan." He clapped him on the back. "And Chloe. You look great."

A tinge of pink colored her cheeks. "Hi, Jason. It's been a while."

Jason stepped over and enveloped her in a huge hug.

Aidan stuffed his hands deep into his pockets, fighting the envy that surged through him.

"Jason, go wash up. Dinner will be ready any minute." Maxi tied a bib around Ben's neck.

Jason crossed the room to wrap an arm around his

wife's waist. "Why don't you come and give me a hand?" His suggestive tone made Maxi swat him.

"Behave yourself. We have company."

He laughed and planted a noisy kiss on her lips. "Be right back."

Aidan was glad his sister had found happiness with the man she'd loved since high school, yet part of him wished he could find the same contentment, the same intimate connection.

"Salad's ready." Chloe turned with a huge wooden bowl in her hands.

"Here, let me." He took it from her and set it in the middle of the large kitchen table.

While Maxi ladled chili into hefty bowls, Aidan carried over the utensils and a basket of biscuits. Soon everyone was seated around the table.

While Jason said the blessing, Aidan glanced over at Chloe. Her eyes were closed, her head bowed. She looked every bit a devout Christian. Was Chloe a strong believer like Jason and Maxi? Or did she struggle with her faith like him?

Ever since the fiasco in Arizona, Aidan found himself questioning his beliefs. All his life he'd trusted that if he lived honestly and did the right thing, nothing bad would happen to him. That theory self-destructed pretty fast when a good deed went horribly awry.

His gaze fell on the long sweep of Chloe's lashes against her cheek. The flow of her hair cast a shadow on her face—a face so beautiful it made his heart hurt. The prayer ended, and she opened her eyes, staring right at him. He looked away, mortified to be caught gawking at her like a besotted teenager.

"So, Aidan. How are things at school?"

Aidan focused back on Jason. "The usual. Unruly kids, frazzled teachers. Fairly normal—until the incident this afternoon." He shook his head, recalling the commotion.

"What happened?" Maxi passed him the basket of biscuits.

"Mrs. Merriweather, our home economics teacher, burned herself pretty badly during class. Principal Jenkins had to take her to the hospital in Kingsville."

"That's awful. Will she be all right?"

"I think so. But she won't be able to cook for a while, until her hand heals. We may have to postpone the cooking segment of the curriculum." He stabbed a piece of cucumber in his salad, trying not to think about shuffling the students' schedules around, and then raised a brow at the stillness around the table. "What?"

"I think I know someone who could help." Maxi had that predatory gleam, which meant one thing. *Trouble.*

Chloe's eyes widened, fork suspended in mid-air. Her brows descended into a sharp V. "Absolutely not."

Aidan's gaze toggled back and forth between the two women. "I don't follow."

"Chloe's in between jobs at the moment. Until she finds something else, she'd be perfect to fill in. Who better than a real chef?"

Chloe was out of work? Warning flares flashed in his brain. Being around Chloe more than absolutely necessary would not be a good idea. Not if he wanted to keep this burgeoning attraction at bay. "Aren't you busy helping Nick and Lily with the kids?" he asked.

"Nick hired a nanny today. She's starting on Monday."

Aidan searched for an appropriate response to his sister's sharp gaze, which gouged him like the pointed end of his knife.

Jason, ever the voice of reason, came to the rescue. "No need to decide anything this minute. Maybe Mrs. Merriweather's burn won't be as serious as you think. Or maybe she'll have a solution of her own."

Aidan heaved a sigh of relief. "You're right. No use speculating until we know the facts."

He ducked his head and dug into his chili, pausing to pray that Mrs. Merriweather's injury wasn't as bad as he feared.

5

Chloe followed Myra Goodwin out of the shop on McIntyre Street, her thoughts a chaotic jumble of excitement. The site was perfect for what she had in mind. It already contained the basics she would need for a bakery. A good coat of paint and a few upgrades would at least get her started. However, she would eventually need more specialized ovens and at least one industrial-sized refrigerator. The rent was a little more than she'd hoped, but not outrageous.

"So what do you think?" Myra stopped tapping on her phone long enough to look at Chloe. She pushed her reading glasses up onto her short, silver hair.

"I'm definitely interested," Chloe said. "But I'd need time to apply for a bank loan to cover the startup costs."

Myra frowned. "This is a hot property. How long are we talking?"

Chloe tried not to laugh. Myra made it sound like the place was a coveted condo in downtown Manhattan. "A couple of weeks should do it." Paul owed her severance pay, which Chloe expected any day. Still, she would likely need a small business loan to get going.

Myra considered her for a moment. "I'll tell my client you're interested, but if another offer comes through, I won't be able to hold it." She tapped a finger on her phone. "I guess I could let you know if that happens."

"Thank you so much." Chloe held out her hand.

Myra shook it. "I'll be in touch. Let me know if you get the funding."

"I will."

Chloe mulled her options as she walked. Her best source of money—the one she'd planned to use for a business one day—was her trust fund. After her mother died, their family home had been sold and all investments reverted to her estate, which Chloe wouldn't have access to until she turned twenty-five. Almost two years away. But as executor of the estate and guardian of her trust, Nick had the power to overrule that stipulation. Should she ask him for some of the money now?

Nick would never hand over the money without a detailed explanation.

Was she prepared to bare everything? Her stomach clenched with dread. No, she wasn't ready for that type of discussion. A loan seemed her best option.

Chloe headed home to dig out her business plan. With a few tweaks, it would be ready to present to the bank by tomorrow.

~*~

Aidan hung up the office phone and dropped his head into his hands. A dull throbbing pulsed at his temples. Mrs. Merriweather couldn't cook for at least a month. And every replacement he'd called couldn't fill in.

Frustrated, he pulled out a drawer and grabbed a bottle of aspirin.

Mrs. Merriweather had suggested he ask Chloe for

help—cheerfully admitting she'd been prompted by a call from Maxi.

Aidan thought about throttling his meddlesome sister.

Being around Chloe every day was not a good idea given his unwanted attraction. But other than restructuring the entire Home Economics curriculum for this semester, what real choice did he have? He picked up the phone to call Maxi who was more than happy to provide him with Chloe's number.

Fifteen minutes later, Aidan finished the salami sandwich he'd brought for lunch.

A soft rap sounded on the door.

"Come in."

"Hi. The secretary wasn't at her desk." Chloe's amber eyes held a hint of tentativeness. "Am I interrupting?"

"Of course not." He gestured to his guest chair. "Thanks for coming so fast."

He tried not to stare at the gloss of her hair, the perfect cut of her jacket, or the swing of her skirt above another pair of crazy high heels.

"What did you want to see me about?"

He cleared his throat. "I wondered if you'd given any thought to Maxi's idea about helping with the home economics class."

"Not really."

"It turns out Mrs. Merriweather will be side-lined for at least a month."

"Oh, that's too bad." Concern flooded Chloe's features. "Mrs. Merriweather got me interested in being a chef. I can't believe she hasn't retired yet."

"You can't keep that woman down. Even this injury won't stop her for long." He folded his hands.

"Which brings me to her suggestion."

"Oh, what's that?"

"Have an experienced cook come in to do the hands-on portion. Mrs. Merriweather would be there to supervise the kids, prepare the written lessons and tests, that sort of thing. Any chance you'd be interested in helping out for a few weeks?" Why were his palms sweating?

Chloe frowned. "I don't know..."

She'd been adamant about not wanting to do this. But she was out of work, and a cash incentive might help.

"I could pay you a small fee for your time. We usually offer a stipend to anyone who comes in to share their expertise with the kids."

She hesitated. "Actually I'm thinking of starting a new business venture."

"What type of business?"

A smile lit her eyes. "A coffee shop and bakery."

"So you'll be staying in Rainbow Falls?" Why did that thought both excite and terrify him? The knowledge that Chloe would be going back to Manhattan had been the main reason Aidan refused to think about a relationship. That, and the fact he'd sworn off romance for the next fifty years.

Chloe's features hardened. "New York has lost its appeal, believe me."

"Sounds as if you left on unpleasant terms." He softened his voice. "What happened, Chloe?"

Her eyes widened, and a hint of fear flickered. "I needed a change."

He was certain she wasn't telling him the whole story, but kept his expression neutral. "I'm afraid I'll need more than that."

"Why?"

"If you were let go from your job, I need to know the reason. I have to be careful who I expose my kids to."

"You'll have to find someone else." She jumped up.

"Chloe, wait." He rounded the desk. "Won't you reconsider—for Mrs. Merriweather's sake? She needs your help."

Her anguished expression made him feel like the lowest type of heel.

"I don't—"

"She specifically asked for you."

Chloe hesitated. "I'll do it on one condition."

"Which is?"

"What I'm about to tell you is confidential. You have to promise not to tell anyone—not Nick, Lily, or Maxi. When I'm ready, I'll tell them myself."

He held back a barrage of questions and nodded. "Agreed."

They both reclaimed their respective seats.

"So," he began, hoping to put her at ease. "I take it there were problems in the workplace."

She gripped her hands together on her lap. "The problem wasn't with my work. It was personal. I was seeing one of the co-owners of the restaurant—romantically—and the relationship didn't end well. Richard forced his partner to fire me." Color bled into her cheeks.

"That hardly seems fair. Couldn't you sue for wrongful dismissal?"

"There's no point. They have all the power and the legal connections. It wouldn't be worth the time, the money, or the frustration."

Anger hummed through his system at the lingering sadness in her eyes. But it wasn't his battle to fight. "Well, as far as I'm concerned, firing someone for something like that is reprehensible." His dark thoughts spiraled back to his departure from his job in Arizona. It appeared he and Chloe had more in common than he'd imagined.

"Thank you for saying that." She seemed to come to a decision. "If you're still willing to have me, I would like to help Mrs. Merriweather."

"You wouldn't object to having a criminal check done?"

"Not at all."

A wave of relief swept through him. "Great. I'll have Mrs. Merriweather contact you to discuss the plan." With a quick prayer that this wasn't a decision they'd both regret, Aidan rose. "Since you're here, why don't I show you where you'll be working?"

~*~

The school's large industrial kitchen wasn't bad at all. It must have been updated over the years. The stovetops rivaled the fancy ones at *Oliver's*. The ovens were functional, but the huge twin refrigerator made her drool. She'd love one like it in her future bakery.

A couple of students clad in white aprons stood at the sink, washing dishes.

"Hi, Mr. North." One girl waved and smiled.

"Girls." Aidan tipped his head, and then frowned. "What are you doing in here?"

"We thought we'd surprise Mrs. Merriweather and give the kitchen a good cleaning while she's away."

Aidan's taut features relaxed. "That's very thoughtful. It's nice of you to give up your lunch period."

One girl bounded over like an eager puppy. "What's going to happen now, Mr. North? If Mrs. Merriweather can't use her hand, she won't be able to teach us to cook." Her chemically-enhanced blonde hair fluttered around her face.

The second girl, tall and slim, with straight brown hair pulled into a sleek ponytail, remained at the sink, but peered over one shoulder.

"We've just come up with a solution to that particular problem. Daphne, this is Miss Martin. She'll be helping Mrs. Merriweather with the cooking portion of the class. Miss Martin, this is Daphne Sharpe and over there is Lindsay Brown."

Daphne's eyes widened. "You're a teacher?"

"No, actually I'm a chef."

The girl looped the dishtowel over her shoulder. "Shouldn't you be working in a restaurant or something?"

"Daphne." Aidan's warning held a ring of authority.

"I'm out of work at the moment so I have time to spare." Chloe smiled. "Besides, Mrs. Merriweather taught me to cook. Now I have a chance to do something for her."

Lindsay, the quieter girl, came forward, drying her hands on an apron. "You're a real chef?"

The girl's flawless complexion and serious hazel eyes complemented high cheekbones and an upturned nose. Yet an aura of sadness shimmered around her.

"I am. I used to work for a restaurant in New York. Now I'm planning to open a bakery in town."

"I want to be a chef too. Someday."

"I promise to share my best tips with you." Chloe winked. "You'll be a pro in no time."

The hint of a smile hovered on Lindsay's lips and a new mission bloomed in Chloe's mind. Maybe helping Mrs. Merriweather with these students wouldn't be such a bad thing after all.

6

"The new teacher's hot."

Giggles and other adolescent noises followed the declaration behind her.

Chloe didn't react as she wrote her name on the white board.

The culprit had to be one of the five boys in the class. Most likely Dylan, the shaggy-haired Romeo in the first row.

She turned to face the group, hoping Mrs. Merriweather would return from the office before they noticed Chloe's knees shaking. "Hi, everyone. I'll be assisting Mrs. Merriweather with this class for a few weeks."

A wolf whistle erupted.

Chloe needed to gain the upper hand or they'd make tapioca pudding out of her. "Keep in mind that Vice Principal North, or Principal Jenkins, could come in at any time. You don't want to give them any reason to get rid of me, do you?" She pinned Dylan with a no-nonsense stare.

A chorus of no's filled the air.

"Good. So let's keep things professional and we'll get along just fine."

A few girls snickered behind their notebooks.

"I hope you aren't giving Miss Martin a hard time." The no-nonsense voice of Chloe's former teacher preceded her into the classroom. The stout, gray-haired woman frowned at her students. Obviously having her bandaged hand in a sling would not deter her.

"No, ma'am," came the sheepish chorus.

Chloe bit back a smile at the familiar scenario. It was as if she'd never graduated.

"Good. Now let's get started."

After Mrs. Merriweather's lesson, Chloe herded the kids into the kitchen. The teacher had chosen a fairly simple recipe of spaghetti and meat balls.

Soon Chloe had a group boiling noodles, one browning the meatballs, and another making sauce. The appealing scent of onions and garlic filled the room. Chloe kept close to Lindsay, impressed with the girl's skill. Chloe pulled the metal colander over to the sink so that Lindsay could drain the pasta. "Does your mother like to cook, Lindsay?"

"Not really." The girl's response was tight-lipped.

"Is your dad the cook in the family, then?"

Lindsay dropped a ladle into the empty pot with a clunk. "My dad left when I was six."

Chloe stilled. "I'm sorry. That must have been tough."

"Yeah." Lindsay's gaze slid away. "My mom works a lot, so I cook for us."

"Do you have any brothers or sisters?"

"A younger brother." Lindsay reached for a stack of plates on the counter.

Chloe began to get the picture. Lindsay was responsible for her brother while her mother worked long hours. No wonder the girl looked beaten by the world. Chloe's father had died when she was twelve. The sense of loss haunted her childhood, as she was sure it haunted Lindsay.

"I'm sorry things are hard for you at home. But

cooking is great therapy. Whenever I feel sad, I whip up a batch of brownies. Guaranteed to make anyone smile."

Lindsay gave a wistful smile. "I know. Cooking is the best thing in my life."

Chloe hoped to inspire Lindsay with dreams for the future, just as Mrs. Merriweather had done for her.

After the final bell sounded, Chloe scoured the kitchen. Scrubbing out the deep, stainless steel sink, she realized with a start that she hadn't thought of Richard in hours. Keeping busy was proving to be the best medicine.

Voices echoed from the hallway, and the door squeaked open.

Chloe turned, expecting to see Mrs. Merriweather.

Instead, Aidan strode toward her.

Her heart thumped a hard beat in her chest. Handsome and authoritative in his navy suit, his presence dominated the room.

He leaned one hip against the counter and smiled. "So how was the first day?"

She continued to wipe the counters. "Better than I expected. So far the kids are well behaved."

He raised an eyebrow. "Even Dylan Moore? He can be a handful."

"I think we've reached an understanding. For now." She hung the cloth over the sink to dry.

"How are you getting home?"

"I planned to walk. It's a beautiful day." Her pulse skittered at his intense gaze.

"Can I give you a ride? There's something I'd like to show you on the way. A project I have in mind for the kids."

The pull of attraction quivered along her nerve

endings like a living, breathing being. Chloe pushed a piece of hair behind one ear, wishing she could push her feelings away as easily. The need for caution warred with her curiosity. What kind of project did he have in mind? Could it help her get to know Lindsay better? Although she wanted—no, *needed*—to keep her distance from Aidan, the ride would give her the chance to ask him more about the girl.

"Wait one minute and I'll get my purse."

~*~

Aidan pulled into the lot adjacent to the abandoned building. Nerves, along with his afternoon coffee, churned in his stomach. Getting Chloe on board with this project would mean spending more time around her, a potential problem unless he could get his feelings under control. He didn't need a romantic involvement with any woman, much less a co-worker and his sister's best friend.

But to get his venture underway, he needed someone with Chloe's energy and enthusiasm. Most of the teachers on staff were more interested in retirement than in taking on any extra-curricular activities with the kids.

"Isn't this the old YMCA?" Chloe asked.

"It is. Come in, and I'll show you my plan."

The run-down building would need a fair bit of work, but Aidan could envision the end result with perfect clarity. He unlocked the front door. The rusty hinges groaned.

"How come you have a key?" Wariness swam in Chloe's brown eyes.

"The owner is a friend of mine. He let me have the

key to see if the space would suit for a teen rec center I want to open." Aidan flipped the light switch, illuminating a swarm of dust motes.

In the large room that functioned as a gymnasium, basketball nets hung on either side of the area. A set of bleachers took up one wall. A faint odor of old gym shoes hung in the air.

"This space would be great for all types of sports." Aidan led the way to a door at the far end, pushed it open, and turned on the light. "And I thought I could turn this into a games room, where the kids could read, watch TV, or play video games. I'll add a couple of couches, maybe an area rug. I'd want to paint it and make it brighter, more welcoming." He stopped rambling long enough to gauge her reaction. "What do you think?"

She scanned the room. "It's a great idea. Who would supervise the kids when they're here?"

Aidan shrugged. "That's one of the details I haven't worked out yet. I was hoping to get input from any teachers or parents who may want to volunteer their time."

Chloe walked around the perimeter. "You could get a Ping-Pong table in here. Kids would love that. And ask for donations of used games and books. You could have a table and chairs on this side. And maybe an Internet station."

He smiled. She was getting enthused about the project, just as he'd hoped. "Exactly. Somewhere they can kick back and relax, without getting into trouble."

"Reminds me of the youth group Nick used to run in the church basement when I was a teen. Nick forced me to go—for my own good." She grinned. "I went through a rebellious period."

His heart stuttered at her mischievous expression. With considerable effort, he pulled his attention back to the conversation. "My plan is to expand on the idea of a youth group and incorporate more physical activities, like basketball, volleyball, maybe some floor hockey. Something to keep the boys off the street."

"That should work." She stuck her head out the door. "Is there a kitchen in here somewhere?"

"I think so. A small one in the far corner."

"Let's check it out. I could get the kids making snacks. Or maybe offer cooking lessons."

"So you'd be willing to help then?" Aidan tried not to appear too eager as they entered the kitchenette. He snapped on the light, revealing a serviceable area with a stove, an older fridge, a sink and counter, as well as a rectangular workspace in the middle.

"Sure. It sounds worthwhile for the kids." She opened the oven to peer inside. "Speaking of kids, what can you tell me about Lindsay Brown?"

Aidan blinked at the sudden change in topic. "She's a good student. Has a younger brother, Matt, who can be a challenge at times. Why?"

Chloe pulled her jacket tight, reminding Aidan to check the heating system.

"I don't know. She just seems so sad all the time."

Aidan frowned and stepped toward her, close enough to smell her perfume. "Let me give you some advice. It's best to stay out of the students' personal lives."

She bristled like an indignant hen. "How can you say that? Some of these kids need us to get involved. If their parents aren't looking out for them, don't we have an obligation to do so?"

Her unexpected anger took Aidan by surprise. A

bitter swirl of emotion swam in his stomach as the image of Emily Andrews came to mind. "Not everyone wants to be helped, Chloe. Sometimes it's best to leave well enough alone." He'd learned the hard way that good intentions did not always count when things went wrong. He switched off the kitchen lights and strode into the gym.

The clatter of Chloe's high-heeled boots warned him she wasn't about to let this go. Her hand on his arm stopped him, as did her amber eyes, which burned bright.

"What happened to make you so cynical?"

He pulled his arm free and paced away, stopping with his back to her. He closed his eyes against the tide of memories sweeping in. Loathe as he was to talk about the past, he needed to make Chloe understand the dangers involved. He turned to face her. "I used to be like you when I first started teaching. That changed when I tried to help one of my students, a troubled sixteen-year-old girl named Emily." He paused to contain his emotions. "She confided in me, told me she was being abused by a family member. I tried to intervene. Called in Child Protective Services…and got punched out by her father for my efforts." He rubbed his jaw, remembering the unpleasant sensation. "After several sessions with a social worker, the girl finally admitted she had lied to get my attention. Turns out she had some romantic delusions about me." He forced back the anger he still carried. "I got suspended for trying to help someone I thought was in trouble."

"I'm sorry. That's so unfair."

"The point is you need to keep things strictly professional. Let the school counselors handle anything else." What did he see in her eyes? Sadness, confusion, regret?

"I'm sorry, I don't know if I can do that," she said softly. "But I'll keep it in mind."

Her phone chirped out some pop tune. She pulled it out, grimaced at the display, and stuffed it back in her pocket.

"Aren't you going to answer that?"

"No." Color tinged her cheeks.

"Your boyfriend?" The words came out too harsh.

"*Ex*-boyfriend."

"Does he call often?"

"Yes, but I don't answer." She pushed out the front door.

Aidan turned off the main lights, locked the door, and then followed her to the car.

Chloe sat, staring straight ahead.

He slid into the driver's side, hating the unspoken tension. "What did he do?" Aidan's question was quiet as he pulled onto the street.

Her phone chimed again.

When she accepted the call, he frowned. She'd rather talk to the jerk than answer him. Not a good sign.

"Richard, I told you to stop calling."

Aidan couldn't make out his response.

"I don't care what…" Chloe rubbed a hand across her forehead. "Nothing has changed, Richard. Don't call again." She disconnected with a loud huff and crammed the device into her purse.

Aidan let a minute pass in silence. "He wants you back, doesn't he?" *What guy wouldn't?*

"It doesn't matter. It's far too late for that."

7

At the loud rapping, Chloe looked up from the book of recipes. Who would drop by unannounced on a Sunday afternoon? Maybe Aidan wanted to borrow a cup of sugar. Did she have any sugar? Her heart rattled against her ribcage. She set the book aside, wishing she was dressed in something other than old jeans and a sweatshirt. She smoothed her hair down, wet her lips, and opened the door. "Nick. What are you doing here?"

Her cousin's normally cheery disposition was eclipsed by his glare. "I need to talk to you, Chloe. If you're not too busy." The last words dripped with sarcasm. Was he mad at her?

"I'm never too busy for you. Come in." Her mind raced over any possible offences. Had she not been nice enough to the new nanny? No, she and Mrs. Smythe had got on just fine when they met. Chloe couldn't think of a thing she'd done to deserve Nick's displeasure.

Then realization dawned. It was Sunday, and she hadn't attended church service. *Again.* Her cousin, the minister, would expect her to be there. She led him to the living room with a guilty heart. "Can I get you something to drink? A snack?"

"No, thank you." He perched on the edge of the large, green armchair and gestured for her to take a seat.

Maybe if she dove right in, she could diffuse the situation. "So how was church today?"

"Fine. Not that you'd know, since you haven't bothered to attend one service since you've been home." His blond brows cinched together. "This isn't like you, Chloe. You never used to miss church on Sunday. Has New York changed you that much?"

How could she tell him she didn't feel worthy to step into the Lord's house? "Sorry. I—I overslept."

"Stop it."

Her head jerked up at the harshness of his words. Suddenly, she was fifteen again, facing Nick's wrath over her rebellious actions. When Chloe's father died, Nick had stepped in to take over as the man of the household. She hadn't always appreciated his interference. *Like now.*

"I want to know what's happened to you. Why you're acting so different since you've come home. And why you're working at the high school. What happened to your job in New York?" The worry in his eyes masked the anger.

Apparently Lily hadn't shared her concerns with Nick about Chloe's lack of employment.

"I left *Oliver's*." She crossed to the fireplace to fiddle with a picture frame on the mantel.

"Why would you do that? I thought it was your dream job."

"A difference of opinion got...out of hand. Anyway, I'm home, so it all turned out for the best."

"Not good enough." Nick turned her to face him. "I want to know what Richard did to you. And don't tell me this isn't about him, because I'm not buying it."

Blazing eyes bored into hers. Love fueled his anger, she knew. A love she cherished all the more now that Nick and Lily were her only family.

"If I tell you, you'll want to hurt him, so I think it's best you don't know the details." *Coward.* It was better for *her* if he didn't know the details.

"Did he hit you?"

"No."

"He cheated on you, didn't he?"

Unable to bear his scrutiny, she moved to the window where a soft breeze lifted the lace curtain. "Not in the way you think."

"How then?"

She braced for his reaction. "I found out Richard is married."

Nick's brows shot skyward. "Married? You mean separated?"

"Not exactly." Chloe hugged her arms. "But he swore he was planning to leave his wife when the time was right."

"Isn't that a convenient answer?" A nerve pulsed in Nick's jaw. "So he used you, had a good time at your expense, then cast you aside when he got bored?"

"It wasn't like that." How could she explain it when even she didn't understand? Chloe searched for something to say. "Look, I'm not the first person to get mixed up in a bad relationship. It's over now, and I need some time to recover." She tried the same pleading look she'd used on him as a teenager when he'd caught her doing something wrong. Maybe it would still work.

He blew out an exasperated breath. "You're asking for space?"

"That would be helpful, yes."

He paced as though gathering his thoughts, and then finally looked at her. "What are you going to do now? For work, I mean."

"I'm thinking of starting my own business." As she explained, the lines in his face gradually relaxed.

"I don't know how much call there is for a bakery in town, but if anyone can make a go of it, you can." He smiled. "I'm sorry about everything that's happened, but I'm very glad you're home to stay." He opened his arms.

Chloe stepped into his warm embrace, relief spilling through her tense muscles. The great thing about Nick was he didn't stay mad long.

When she pulled away, he held her by the shoulders. "Remember, Chloe, in times of crisis, it's best to bring your problems to God, not hide from Him. I expect to see you in church next Sunday."

Her momentary relief faded. "I'll do my best."

~*~

"Good job, everyone. Cleanup starts now." Chloe stuffed her hands into the pocket of her white apron.

The eating portion of the class was over, and now the dreaded dish duty began. They had made an excellent beef stroganoff, complete with salad and dessert, and had just finished enjoying the fruits of their labor. The eager students, ones like Lindsay, Ellen and Daphne, jumped up to clear the dishes.

Tommy, a lanky redhead, patted his stomach. "This class was the best idea ever."

Chloe chuckled. "Glad you're enjoying it, Tommy. If you work as hard at washing the dishes as you did eating the food, you'll be on your way to an A, I'm sure."

Tommy made an exaggerated leap for the sinks.

Chloe started to stack the plates and caught herself humming. After two weeks in Mrs. Merriweather's class, Chloe could honestly say she'd never felt this content. Working at *Oliver's* had been exciting, but catering to the clientele every night got tiresome. And the stress eventually caught up to everyone. Here, the immense satisfaction she gained from watching the kids master a skill was a surprise to her. She even had a few star chefs in the making.

Lindsay Brown was one of them.

Chloe's gaze strayed to her pet student as Lindsay loaded the industrial-sized dishwasher. Dylan Moore stood right beside her, close enough that his hand strayed to her hip. A telltale pink tinged Lindsay's cheeks as she cast a shy smile over her shoulder.

Warning bells rang in Chloe's head. Visions of Richard doing the same thing to her when he first started hanging around the kitchen at *Oliver's* flooded her brain.

"Mr. Moore, I'm sure Lindsay can load the dishes by herself. Why don't you get a towel and dry those pots?" She folded her arms and waited.

He glared, whispered something to Lindsay, and then grudgingly moved toward the sink.

Lindsay darted a quick look at Chloe before returning to her task.

When the kitchen had been returned to its normal state, Chloe turned her attention to Lindsay, thankful to find her alone. Chloe wanted to get the girl's mind on something else besides a certain boy. "Lindsay, have you ever heard of the Junior Chef Challenge?"

The girl wrung out the rag over the sink. "I don't think so."

"It's a cooking contest, held once a year. Students

compete for a scholarship to a leading culinary school. From what I've seen of your skills, I think you'd have a good chance of winning."

The girl's eyes widened. A glimpse of joy bloomed before her expression darkened. "There's no point in entering, Miss Martin. Even if I won, I couldn't leave home." She scrubbed the counter with more vigor than necessary.

"I'm sure your mother wants you to get a good education. To follow your passion."

"It doesn't matter. I can't abandon my brother that way. My mother works two jobs, and without me around, Matt would get into trouble for sure."

Chloe put a gentle hand on Lindsay's shoulder. "Are you willing to sacrifice your dreams for your brother?" she asked softly.

Lindsay lifted her chin. "If that's what it takes, then yes."

Lindsay hung up her apron and walked into the hallway where Dylan stood waiting. The boy took her hand as they left.

Chloe sighed. The girl's decision not to attend college might have more to do with a certain shaggy-haired senior than her brother.

8

Standing outside the door to the recreation center on Saturday morning, Aidan whistled to get the motley crowd's attention. All heads swiveled in his direction. "I want to thank everyone for coming out today. Your help will go a long way in getting this place ready for our new youth center. When I open the door, I want everyone to divide into teams and await further instructions inside."

Aidan flung the door wide and stood back while the teens poured by. He shook his head, awed that more than twenty kids had shown up to help paint the gymnasium and games room. His dream was slowly becoming a reality, and he had Chloe to thank for it.

"Are you going to stand there all day or start painting?" Chloe grinned and plopped a baseball cap on her head, pulling her long ponytail through the opening.

"I can't believe you got this many kids to come out," Aidan said as they entered the building. "How'd you do it?"

Her smile grew wider, creating an enchanting dimple in one cheek. "Easy. I bribed them with food. Pizza and homemade cookies. Works every time."

"Why didn't I think of that?"

Her bright laugh echoed as she headed over to join one of the groups.

Aidan squashed the urge to follow her and crossed

the room in the other direction.

The teens divided themselves into five groups of four with a couple of stragglers.

He picked one crew to work on the games room while the rest he assigned to a different wall in the gym.

Chloe took Lindsay and Daphne into the kitchen to start scrubbing the appliances.

At least she was out of sight for the time being. Saved him the distraction.

Three hours of sweat and effort later, the crew broke for lunch.

Chloe brought out several large pizzas and a container of cookies.

"You made the pizza?"

"Not just me. The kids helped yesterday after class. And I made the cookies last night at home."

He snagged one of the sweets. "That's what smelled so good. Every time I went out into the hall, I could smell something incredible."

Her beaming smile melted his insides, while the cookie melted on his tongue. He'd certainly be a customer at any bakery she opened.

The kids took their food out to the gym. Aidan grabbed a slice of pizza and started to follow the others, but stopped at Chloe's scowl.

She was staring into the gym, her mouth pinched.

"Is something wrong?"

"Dylan Moore is making moves on Lindsay."

He peered over her shoulder, trying to ignore the rush of her floral perfume.

Dylan sat beside Lindsay, feeding her bites of pizza.

"And this poses a problem for you?"

She whirled to face him so fast their noses almost touched. "Lindsay's a sensitive girl. And I know Dylan's type. He'll dump her as soon as someone prettier comes along."

"How do you know this after only two weeks with the kids?"

"Oh, come on, Aidan. Dylan's reputation is hardly a secret."

He set his plate down on the nearest surface. "And Lindsay is perfectly aware of it. If she chooses to go out with him, that's her decision."

Chloe's brows shot together. "Even if she's throwing away her future?"

Exasperation spurted through him. "How does a teenage crush translate to Lindsay throwing away her future?"

Chloe moved to the counter and started to box up the leftovers. "She's not even considering going to college and I think Dylan is a big part of the reason."

Aidan banked down his irritation and kept his tone level. "I told you, Chloe, you can't get involved in these kids' lives. The best you can do is offer advice. Whether they choose to take it or not is up to them."

She turned blazing eyes on him. "Sorry, that's not good enough. I can't sit by and watch a talented girl throw her life away."

Though Aidan admired her passion and her dedication to the students, he couldn't agree with her methods. But arguing with her would get him nowhere. With an inward sigh, he headed into the gym, vowing to keep a discreet eye on Chloe and hope she didn't do something she'd later regret.

~*~

In the basement of her building, Chloe crammed the sheets into the washing machine, dumped in the soap, and dropped the lid. Her insides still hummed with frustration after her conversation with Aidan.

How could he care enough about children to work in the education industry, and even start a youth center to help them, but ignore their personal problems with such ease? It didn't make any sense.

She punched the button to start the washer and then bent to pull her clothes from the dryer. Maybe Aidan could turn a blind eye, but she couldn't. If it took every trick she had, she'd get Lindsay to enter that cooking competition.

Her cellphone vibrated. She pulled it out and accepted the call.

"Chloe? It's Myra Goodwin. I'm calling to check on your status regarding the shop on McIntyre Street. I have another customer interested in the property."

"Just a minute, Myra. I can't hear you very well." Chloe's stomach dipped. She hadn't expected this, mainly because the store had been empty for months.

Chloe stepped into the hallway away from the noisy machine, mentally calculating the total in her bank account now that her severance pay had been deposited. She'd presented her business plan to Mr. Johnson, the bank manager, and filled out her loan application. He'd promised he would make his decision early next week. Though fairly confident he'd grant her request, she couldn't go ahead without that extra security. Yet she wasn't about to let this property slip through her fingers. "I should hear from Mr. Johnson about the loan by Monday or Tuesday." If the bank turned her down, she'd be forced to approach

Nick about her trust fund. Still, she had no idea how long it would take once Nick approved the idea.

Silence hummed over the phone. "That's too bad. I'm not sure there's anything I can do if my client accepts this other offer."

Chloe's spirits sank. "I understand. Please let me know what happens."

"I'll call you on Monday with an update."

Chloe bit back her disappointment. She'd had her heart set on that location. Everything about it was perfect. Well, no matter. If she didn't get it, she'd find somewhere else. Nothing would deter her, now that she'd made up her mind.

The sound of rushing water snapped her to attention. She pushed open the door and her optimistic mood vanished. The washing machine choked and gasped, spewing soapy water onto the floor like an erupting volcano.

"No. No. I do not need this right now." Chloe skated through the water and bubbles. She hauled her basket of clean clothes onto the old wooden table and then turned to face the vomiting washer. No matter how she twisted the dials or banged the lid, nothing stopped the flow.

"Where is the shut-off for this thing?"

Water seeped through her sneakers and socks. She found taps down the wall behind the machine. Could she reach them without pulling the whole thing out? Her soaked sweatshirt and jeans stuck to her skin. She climbed on top of the washer and stretched. If only her arms were a few inches longer. Without warning, her knees slid sideways on the slick surface. She cried out as she battled to regain her balance...and lost.

9

Aidan scrolled his mouse over the webpage for *Oliver's Emporium* in New York and clicked on the tab marked "Staff." Second from the top, he found a picture of a smiling Chloe in a white chef coat and hat.

He clicked the page closed and set his laptop on the coffee table. Raking his hand through his hair, he blew out a disgusted breath. He'd been reduced to spying on the woman in cyberspace. Clearly, he was losing all perspective when it came to Chloe Martin. Hyper-aware of her every movement, his ears were constantly attuned to every creak on the staircase, every step in the hall. Seventeen minutes ago, she had gone down to the laundry room in the basement. It had taken all his willpower not to follow her and rewash his already clean clothes. *Pathetic.* He needed some fresh air to clear his head and focus on something other than his captivating neighbor. Aidan grabbed his jacket from the hook and was looking for his keys when a scream echoed in the hallway. His heart jump-started in his chest. *Chloe!* He raced out of his apartment and down the basement stairs.

A stream of water leaked from under the laundry room door.

Not good. He jumped over the river and pushed the door open.

Inside, the washing machine spouted water like a fountain. Beyond it, a set of limbs flailed in all directions.

Aidan blinked, and then had to bite his lip to keep from laughing out loud.

Chloe was stuck in the laundry tub. "Don't just stand there. Help me out of here."

"How did—"

"Never mind. Turn the taps off first. They're behind the washer."

He waded into the flood, wincing at the cold slosh of wetness invading his shoes. Thirty seconds later, the stream of water stopped. He grinned down at a bedraggled Chloe. "This reminds me of the night you arrived. The wet look suits you."

"Don't you dare laugh! I'm stuck in here." She held out her hand, her expression murderous.

"I think I'll call you Hurricane Chloe from now on." He reached out, trying hard not to laugh.

"Very funny." She smacked him on the arm.

"Hey, the princess does not assault the knight in shining armor. That's not how the story goes." He put his arms around her and lifted her out of the tub, not even caring when her soggy clothes soaked his shirt. "If I remember my fairy tales correctly, the damsel in distress usually rewards her rescuer with a kiss."

The atmosphere in the room changed instantly.

Chloe stopped squirming, her eyes widening in awareness.

The word ricocheted in his head, causing his heart to beat an uneven thump. The fruity scent of her shampoo enveloped him, and his gaze fell to the fullness of her slightly parted lips.

The sound of her quick breath stirred his blood. Mesmerized, he drew closer and touched his mouth to hers. Her lips tasted warm and sweet, like honey with a hint of mint. A mewling sound vibrated from her throat, and she wrapped one arm around his neck, pulling him nearer. The blood thundered in his ears, blocking out all sound, while one hand explored the silkiness of her hair. The world shrank down to the taste of her, the feel of her in his arms. He wished this headiness could go on forever.

A cacophony of music from her cellphone brought reality crashing back.

She dragged her mouth away. "Put me down. I have to get this call."

Dazed, he dropped her feet into the water.

She pulled the phone out and turned her back.

Trying to subdue his riotous pulse, Aidan scrubbed a hand over his face.

What had he just done?

~*~

Chloe leaned on the mop and blew some wisps of hair off her face.

Aidan was wringing out towels in the laundry tub.

She wet her lips, recalling with vivid clarity the taste of their kiss. Heat snaked up her neck into her cheeks. What had she been thinking, kissing him like that? Thank goodness Lily had called before things had gotten out of hand. Chloe raised her head and her mouth went dry.

Aidan's eyes were dark with some raw emotion she couldn't define.

"Do you think it's safe to try the washer now?" She forced lightness into her tone. "I'd like those sheets for tonight."

"We need to talk about what happened." He

moved closer, sending her pulse into a frenzy.

She turned to the basket of clothes and began to fold. "It was a silly response to a silly situation. No harm done." *Yeah, right.* That kiss had rocked her world off its axis, but she'd never admit it.

The heat of his hand on her arm made her still. "It was more than that, and you know it."

She refused to look at him. One glance into those eyes and she'd be lost.

"No matter how spectacular, that kiss was a mistake," he said. "It can't happen again."

He thought the kiss had been spectacular? *A spectacular mistake apparently.*

Anger bubbled up, safe and familiar. Anger she could deal with. "What do you mean a mistake?"

"Mr. Jenkins frowns on anyone getting...involved...in the workplace. Something I happen to agree with. I know from personal experience it never ends well."

"I guess you should've thought of that sooner, Mr. Vice Principal." With a jerk, she hiked the laundry basket onto her hip and stalked out. When she reached her apartment, she fumbled with the door, pushed inside, and dumped the basket on the floor. Why was she so upset over a silly kiss?

Because, as Aidan said, it had been spectacular.

Totally different from the kisses she'd shared with Richard.

What was wrong with her? She'd barely ended one disastrous relationship. How could she even entertain the idea of another romance so soon? Chloe kicked off her sodden shoes and socks and stomped to the bedroom.

"That kiss was a mistake. It can't happen again."

Aidan was right. Not only was she emotionally unprepared for another relationship, she certainly wouldn't start one with Maxi's brother. Chloe wouldn't let anything come between her and her best friend. No kiss—no matter how good—was worth that.

10

Chloe's bad mood had not improved by the next day. Seated in the front row of the Good Shepherd Church, in the pew reserved for family of the clergy, she dared not look around. If she met anyone's eyes, they might discern the truth—that the pastor's cousin was nothing but a fraud. An adulteress, who didn't deserve to be in this holy place, listening to Nick's soothing words of love and forgiveness.

Chloe shifted in her seat, the bench too hard beneath her. Her gaze fell on the spot where Mama had always sat, and a wave of sorrow coursed through her. The last time Chloe had been in this pew had been for Mama's funeral. Was that the reason she hadn't been home since?

The air in the church became too close. Chloe struggled to get oxygen into her lungs. *Please don't let me have a panic attack now.* She'd been doing so well, with only the one small episode the night of the thunderstorm. She'd thought the attacks had been a product of her stressful life in New York. Apparently she was wrong about that too.

Just when Chloe thought she'd go mad, the service ended. Not waiting for the final hymn to finish, she exited out the side door. In the shade of an oak tree, she began deep, even breathing, hoping to circumvent a full-blown attack. Repressed grief rose inside her, adding to the load of guilt she carried. In New York, it had been easy to push aside her memories of Mama, but here in her mother's favorite place, it all came rushing back. *Mama, I miss you so much.* The tears she'd held at bay for the whole service now brimmed on her lashes and spilled over. A movement caught Chloe's attention. She wiped her face and straightened in time to face Maxi and Jason.

"Hey, are you OK?" Maxi's keen eyes missed nothing.

Chloe sniffed. "Just thinking about my mom."

Maxi drew her into a hug. "Oh, honey. I'm so sorry. Is this the first time in church since her funeral?"

Chloe nodded and melted into Maxi's embrace. After a few seconds, she pulled back.

"Why don't you come over for lunch?" Jason asked, little Ben wriggling in his arms.

"Thanks, but I'm supposed to be going to Lily's." Maybe she'd get in the car and go wherever it took her instead. Just keep driving until her emotions settled.

Maxi patted her arm. "OK. But we'll talk soon. I want to hear all about this bakery of yours. It sounds wonderful."

Chloe managed a halfhearted smile, her bruised spirits lifting. Then she looked over Maxi's shoulder and saw Aidan. Her knees turned to rubber. In her present vulnerable state, she could not deal with him. When her phone chose that moment to ring, she was more than happy to answer it.

~*~

Aidan's stomach clenched when Chloe's eyes met his and she turned away. How had things gone so terribly wrong between them? Never had he been so

71

twisted up over a woman. He'd even broken one of his own rules yesterday by kissing her. When he'd returned to Rainbow Falls, he swore if he ever got involved romantically again, it would be with a devout woman, one without lies or schemes, not like his ex-girlfriend, Patricia. Or Chloe Martin—another woman full of secrets.

Still, he couldn't seem to tear his traitorous eyes away from her.

Her dark hair was swept up off her face, baring her neck. A knee-length dress showcased her shapely legs, which ended in some kind of strappy shoe. High heels, of course. And once again she had her cellphone glued to her ear.

Maxi punched his arm. "What's got you in such a bad mood?"

"Nothing." He practically growled at her.

"I'll be right there, Lindsay. Don't move." Chloe's raised voice held a hint of desperation.

Aidan's mood deteriorated even further. Despite his repeated warnings, Chloe had become far too involved in Lindsay Brown's life. With a grunt, he pushed past his sister to intercept Chloe before she could escape. "What was that about?"

Chloe shot him a glare that could have peeled bark from the tree. "None of your business."

"I'm making it my business." He stepped closer. "Is Lindsay in some kind of trouble?"

"What do you care? It's after school hours." She marched past him toward the parking lot.

His chest tightened, and he curled his fingers into his palms. How did she make him laugh one minute and want to throttle her the next? He jogged after her, and before she could get in her car, slapped a hand on the driver's door. "You might as well tell me. I'll just follow you."

Sparks shot from amber eyes that had darkened to a whiskey color. "Stay out of this, Aidan. It's between Lindsay and me."

"Fine. I'll follow you then." He walked toward his car.

"You can't stop me from helping her," she called.

He kept going.

Angry footsteps tapped the pavement. "Wait."

He turned around. Why hadn't he noticed her red eyes? Had she been crying?

"It's Lindsay's brother, Matt. He's in some kind of trouble over at Cooper's store."

Aidan's neck muscles cinched, and he blew out a breath. "I'll go with you."

"You can't. Lindsay called me in confidence." Chloe laid a tense hand on his arm. "Please don't do that to her—or to me."

Aidan wished he could ignore the plea in her voice.

"Chloe, there you are. I've been looking everywhere." Nick frowned as he approached them. "Is there a problem?"

A hint of panic crossed Chloe's features. Her gaze darted to Aidan, practically begging for his help.

Aidan made a decision he hoped he wouldn't regret later. He stared right at her as he answered Nick's question. "Nothing Chloe can't handle."

The relief and gratitude that swept over her face were his reward.

"Tell Lily I'll be over as soon as I clear this up." Chloe opened the car door as she spoke. "An hour tops."

She jumped in and shut the door before Nick could object.

When her car roared away, Nick aimed a suspicious glare at Aidan. "What's going on with you two?"

Aidan pushed back a wave of guilt at the memory of their kiss. "Just trying to give Chloe some advice, which she continues to ignore. She's some kind of stubborn, that one."

Nick's scowl relaxed into a chuckle. "Tell me about it. Ever since Uncle Leonard died, I've tried my best to fill in for him, but it hasn't been easy."

Aidan clapped a hand on Nick's shoulder. "I feel for you, buddy. I really do."

~*~

Chloe parked in front of Cooper's Convenience Store and ran inside.

The store was exactly how she remembered it. The same smell of candy, gum, and pine air freshener. Even the display of magazines remained in the same spot as when she was a teen.

Behind the counter, Mr. Cooper stood frowning at Lindsay. The stout man wore a canvas apron with the words "Cooper's Convenience" in bold red letters. In the corner, a tousled-haired teen sat on a stool, his face as white as the wall behind him.

"Hi, Lindsay. Hello, Mr. Cooper."

Lindsay moved toward Chloe, her face a mirror of anxiety. "Miss Martin, thanks for coming so fast."

Chloe laid a steadying hand on the girl's arm. "It'll be OK. Why don't you let me talk with Mr. Cooper for a minute?"

Lindsay's pinched features relaxed as she went to join her brother.

Chloe turned to the disgruntled man behind the counter. "Mr. Cooper, could I have a word with you, please?"

"What does this have to do with you?" His scowl did nothing to inspire confidence.

"Lindsay is one of my students. I'd like to help if I can."

The man's stiff posture deflated slightly. "You're wasting your time. I've caught the boy trying to steal from me before."

Chloe wished she had some sense of the dynamics in this situation. All she could do was trust her instincts. "What happened today?"

"I saw him in the mirror." He gestured to the round mirror bolted to the wall near the ceiling. "He was shoving some cans of beer into his back pack."

Chloe fought to hide her dismay. Stealing and drinking under age. Not a good sign. "Did he actually leave the store with it?"

"No, because I grabbed him right away. But if I hadn't caught him, he'd have taken the whole lot."

Lindsay and Matt seemed embroiled in a heated conversation of their own.

"What did you do then?"

"I phoned the boy's home. Figured I'd give his mother fair warning before I called Chief Hillier."

"What did Mrs. Brown say?"

"Couldn't reach her. Got Lindsay instead." He shook his graying head. "She begged me to wait until she got here before calling the police. The next thing I knew, you arrived."

Chloe prayed for guidance. Matt's future might

depend on her words. "Is there any way you'd consider not involving the police?"

He shook his head. "I don't know…"

"What if I promised Matt would make restitution for his mistakes? Do some community service?" She warmed to her own idea. "He could work here to make up for the trouble he's caused you."

"I doubt that would be enough of a deterrent."

Matt was the perfect candidate for the youth center. Exactly the sort of kid Aidan was trying to keep out of trouble. "What if I could get someone from Matt's school involved to supervise Matt's community service? Would that help?" She gave Mr. Cooper her most pleading smile.

He huffed out a loud breath. "Well, maybe if the principal agreed to it…"

"How about the vice-principal? Mr. North is opening a youth center to keep the kids off the streets and out of trouble. If we get Matt involved in fixing the place up, he might feel more connected to the center and actually use it."

Mr. Cooper's lips twisted into a reluctant smile. "If Mr. North is half as enthusiastic as you are, young lady, his idea will be a smashing success. You have him call me and we'll see. For now, I'll hold off bringing the police into it. But if anything like this happens again, I'll have no choice."

11

Chloe drove Lindsay and Matt to their apartment. Situated over a run-down dry cleaning store in a poor section of town, the building did not inspire high hopes for the state of the residence above it. Chloe insisted on walking the kids upstairs, wanting to see for herself whether Mrs. Brown was home.

Lindsay barely let her inside the door, claiming that her mother would be back later that night once her job in Kingsville had finished.

The brief view of the cluttered interior confirmed Chloe's worst fears and did nothing to improve her mood. However, there was nothing she could do about it, so after Matt stomped off to his room, Chloe said goodbye to Lindsay and headed home. Disappointment seeped through her as she pulled into her driveway. She would have to call Lily and apologize for missing lunch.

Chloe trudged up the porch stairs, anxious to get out of her high heels and relax in a hot bath. In the main hallway, she hesitated. As much as she wanted to avoid Aidan, she really needed to talk with him about Matt. Give him some advance warning in case Mr. Cooper called him. Before she could change her mind, she marched over and knocked on his door.

Aidan appeared, looking disheveled. "Chloe. Is everything all right with Lindsay and Matt?" He tucked the tail of his shirt into the navy pants he'd been wearing at church earlier.

"That's what I wanted to talk to you about, if you have a minute."

"Sure. Come in." He opened the door wider. "Have a seat."

"No, thanks. I can't stay long." Now that she was here, the idea didn't seem as good. His nearness evoked images of the kiss they'd shared and stirred feelings she'd rather keep buried. "First I want to thank you for helping me with Nick. He's too protective at times."

"You're welcome, though I still don't agree with you being so involved with the kids."

Great. And now she was trying to get *him* involved. "Maybe I will sit down after all." She sank onto the couch and gathered her courage. "I have a favor to ask."

"Why do I get the feeling I won't like this?" Aidan sighed and sat across from her. "This has something to do with the Brown kids, I presume."

"Yes." She gave him a quick run-down. "So I thought having Matt do some community service might serve a dual purpose. Keep Mr. Cooper from having Matt arrested, and possibly get Matt interested in the youth center. After all, he's exactly the type of kid we want to help."

His intense gaze unnerved her.

"If you think it's a bad idea, I—"

"I think it's brilliant."

Her mouth dropped open. "You do?"

"Yes. This might be the very thing that turns Matt around. In any event, it's worth a try. I'm just amazed Mr. Cooper went along with it."

"It took some convincing, but when I mentioned

Matt giving Mr. Cooper some free labor to make up for the trouble he'd caused, he seemed to warm up to the idea. He made it clear though, that this was Matt's last chance. If there's a next time, he will press charges."

"Sounds fair. What about Mrs. Brown? Was she there?"

"No. Apparently she works over in Kingsville and isn't allowed personal calls. That's why Lindsay called me."

He pinned her with a thoughtful stare, one that made her pulse sprint. "I may not agree with your methods, but I have to admit what you're doing for Matt is admirable."

She looked into his handsome face, trying to gauge his sincerity. "Is that a compliment? I couldn't quite tell."

Aidan smiled. "Yes, Chloe. It's a compliment." He paused. "And if you need my help with Matt, I'll do whatever I can."

A boulder of anxiety rolled off her shoulders. "Thanks. I appreciate that." She got up. "Mr. Cooper wants you to call tomorrow. I thought we could get Matt started on a second coat of paint in the gymnasium."

He followed her to the door. "You'll have to supervise Matt during the times he's working."

"I can do that. I'll need a key to the center though."

"Sure. Pick it up whenever you want." When he reached around her to open the door, his arm brushed hers. "Sorry, this door sticks sometimes."

His low voice caused goose bumps to tingle down her neck. She needed to get away before she lost all self-control and did something crazy. Like kissing him again. Ducking under his arm, she escaped into the hallway. "Thanks again. See you at school."

~*~

Mrs. Brown wasn't answering her phone. Aidan would have to call back another time. He scrubbed a hand over his jaw and peered at his watch. Four-thirty. What would Chloe be doing now? He pushed the thought away. As long as Chloe was helping at the school, he had to maintain a professional distance.

His thoughts turned to his ex-girlfriend, and amazingly, the usual sting of betrayal didn't materialize. The hurt he'd suffered at Patricia's hand—her manipulations and ultimate rejection—had lessened, but the bitterness remained. Getting involved with a co-worker had brought a big batch of heartache, and had a negative effect on his career. Aidan wouldn't risk that again. Maybe if he told himself that often enough, he'd start to believe it.

A soft knock sounded, and Chloe poked her head inside. Her brown eyes held a question. "Do you have a minute?"

Aidan's heart took off at a gallop. Her constant presence was making it very hard to ignore her. "Sure. What do you need?"

She stepped inside the room. "I just wanted to tell you that Matt will be working at Mr. Cooper's for the next few days, and we've arranged for him to start at the youth center on Friday. Will that be OK?"

He struggled to focus on her words, not on the way her hair fell in soft waves over her shoulders. "Shouldn't be a problem." He smiled, attempting levity. "What, no hot date for Friday night?"

A hint of color tinted her cheeks. "Nope. I've sworn off dating for the foreseeable future. Besides, I expect to be busy for the next little while."

"OK, I'll bite. Busy how?"

Her eyes literally sparkled. "Getting my bakery ready to open."

"You're kidding? The loan came through?" He knew she'd been waiting for word from the bank.

"Mr. Johnson called me this morning. I went in on my lunch hour and signed the papers." Her excitement filled the room with a palpable energy.

"That's wonderful. Congratulations."

"Thanks. You have no idea how good it feels to get my life back."

He remembered the day he'd got word that he'd been awarded the vice-principal position. "I think I have a fair idea." He smiled. "I'm happy for you, Chloe."

"Thank you. You've been a good friend to me, and I'm grateful."

Friends? Is that what they were?

Their eyes locked, and for a few seconds Aidan forgot to breathe. "Let me get that key for you."

~*~

After work on Wednesday, Chloe unlocked the door and stepped across the threshold of her soon-to-be-bakery. A giddy smile bloomed as she surveyed the property. She still couldn't quite believe the way everything had fallen into place. The person initially wanting the property had decided it didn't meet their needs. When Chloe learned the loan had come through, she'd immediately called Myra and had met with her yesterday to sign the lease. After writing a check for the first and last month's rent, the place was officially hers.

Chloe set down the bucket of cleaning supplies. Excitement bubbled through her system. She'd paint the walls a soothing green and freshen the white of the wicker furniture. The glass display shelves would showcase her confections, and she'd set up a coffee bar on the far side where people could refill their own mugs. She smiled, imagining her customers enjoying themselves in her cozy bistro.

Chloe hummed as she pulled out her little music system, chose her playlist to provide background music, and grabbed some garbage bags. She'd start by getting rid of the trash left by the previous tenant, and then she'd begin scrubbing.

Almost three hours later, she stood back to survey her progress, stretching the tight muscles in her lower back.

The bell over the front door jangled and fresh autumn air blew into the shop.

Aidan stood in the doorway.

At the sight of his tall frame, a thrill of pleasure shot through her. "Aidan. This is a surprise."

"I thought you might be here when I noticed your car wasn't in the driveway."

"You came to check up on me?"

"Maybe." He winked and pulled a bag from behind his back. "I also thought you might be hungry."

"I'm starved. I was so busy, I forgot to eat dinner. What did you bring me?"

"Sandwiches and donuts from Ruby's."

"Chocolate glazed?"

"Of course."

She grinned. "Sounds wonderful."

He dropped the bag, along with take-out coffees, on one of the tables and pulled two wicker chairs around. "Come and sit."

Suddenly conscious of what she must look like in sweats and neon rubber gloves, she held up a finger. "Give me a minute to clean up. Back in a flash." She carried her cleaning supplies to the little bathroom in the back. A glance in the warped mirror over the sink made her grimace. She smoothed her hair, retied her ponytail, and straightened her sweatshirt. It would have to do.

"So this is will be your bakery?" Aidan asked when she re-emerged.

"It will. And a coffee bar as well. The Rainbow Falls answer to a coffee house."

"I like it." He pulled the lid off one of the drinks. "As much as I love Ruby's, her take-out coffee could use some help." He swirled the contents with a stir stick. "You know, these chairs and tables are in pretty good shape. Some white spray paint and they'd be as good as new."

"That's exactly what I have in mind for tomorrow." She picked up half of the sandwich and took a large bite.

"I've got nothing on tomorrow night. I could give you a hand."

"Are you serious?" Even though spending more time with Aidan could prove dangerous to her emotional well-being, her treacherous heart sprinted at the idea.

"It seems only fair after all the work you did at the youth center."

"Then I accept." She pointed to the wall behind

him. "I was hoping to get that wall painted too."

"You bring the paint and I'll be here."

~*~

Aidan whistled as he parked in front of Chloe's shop. Never had he looked so forward to hours of menial labor. Chloe's enthusiasm made every project seem shiny and new. He hoped he could help make her shop look that way too. He got out, popped the trunk, and pulled out drop sheets, paint trays, and rollers. When he entered the front door a few seconds later, his senses were assaulted by a blast of music and the smell of fresh paint. He chuckled.

Chloe liked her music loud while she worked. And she'd been busy. The tables and chairs were covered in old sheets and the first coat of green shone wetly on the far wall.

Aidan wandered to the back of the shop. The rear door to the alley sat wide open. Despite the fact that Rainbow Falls was a safe town, he didn't like Chloe leaving the front door—and the alley door—unlocked when she was here alone.

"Chloe? You here?"

He poked his head into a room and discovered the large, industrial-sized kitchen. He ran his fingers over the stainless steel work area. Not much work needed in here, except a good cleaning.

But where was Chloe?

He strode out of the kitchen and barreled right into her.

She squeaked as the bucket in her hands tilted, sloshing green paint all over her shirt.

He reached out to steady the tin, and his own

hand became covered in green. "Sorry about that."

She laughed. "Good thing it's my favorite color."

"Here, let me get a rag." He took the can and went over to the supplies he'd brought. Setting the pail on a sheet of newspaper, he handed a rag to Chloe and kept one to wipe his hands. "Off to a great start."

She laughed again, her brown eyes sparkling under the rim of an old ball cap. "I'm glad I wasn't the klutz this time."

"Oh, right. I forgot about your bad reputation. Painting with you might be a hazard."

"Risk of the job, buddy." She tossed the rag onto the newspaper and put the lid on the can. "I was about to start the furniture while the first coat on the wall dries."

"OK, tell me what to do."

An hour later, all the wicker pieces had been sprayed.

Aidan stood back and appreciated their handiwork. "Looks as good as I imagined."

"Not bad. Except you missed a spot."

"I did? Where?"

"Right there."

He bent to see where she pointed, and a blast of wetness hit his back.

Her giggle echoed off the walls. "Oops, missed."

The paint seeped down his back.

He turned to find her face contorted with suppressed amusement.

"You did that on purpose."

She doubled up, howling. "Just getting you back for earlier. I think we're even now."

"Oh, we're not even close." He sprinted across the room.

She shrieked and took off running, but he caught up and snagged her around the waist. "You will pay for your treachery."

Chloe squealed again and squirmed in an attempt to escape.

Grinning, he scooped up her legs, and held her pinned to his chest. "I think you'd look good with a nice white mustache."

She doubled her efforts to get free, her breath huffing out between the laughter. Her eyes locked on his with sudden awareness.

He stilled. It was the laundry room all over again. His pulse thudded as his focus fell on her mouth. Those lips—so tempting and close—called to him.

The bell over the door jangled loudly as someone entered.

Chloe jerked in his arms and gasped. "Nick!"

With an inward groan, Aidan released Chloe's feet to the floor.

"What's going on here?" Nick's blue eyes were frostier than his voice.

Aidan swallowed and took a step away from Chloe. "Just a friendly paint fight."

"That's not how it looks from here."

Her cheeks pink, Chloe laid a hand on Nick's arm. "Relax. We were having some fun after a lot of work." She swiped a hand over her forehead. "Come and see what we've done so far."

The harsh lines around Nick's mouth didn't soften. "I think I can see the results from here." He swung his gaze to Aidan. "Looks like I got here just in time."

A trickle of sweat slid down Aidan's back. Nick didn't know how right he was. One more minute and

Aidan might have given in to temptation for a second time.

12

Chloe paused from scrubbing the kitchen in the youth center. Not the ideal way to spend a Friday evening, but since Matt's community service had been her idea, both Aidan and Mr. Cooper had made her responsible for ensuring a dependable adult was present.

Matt rolled paint on the wall, his ever-present earphones glued to his head. For all his grumbling about the work, he really didn't put up much resistance. Mr. Cooper had been impressed with his work ethic, cleaning the storage room and re-stocking the shelves with quiet resolve. And he was turning out to be a pretty good painter as well.

Chloe hummed in time to her own music as she scraped the kitchen counter. She looked at her watch. Another half hour before she could escape to her apartment with a tub of ice cream and a good chick flick. She rinsed the counter and dried her hands.

Matt's slumped shoulders aroused a tug of sympathy. How sad for this fifteen-year-old boy to have no father in his life and a mother who was never home.

The trouble she'd caused her widowed mother when she'd pushed the limits of Mama's patience made her grimace. Thank goodness Nick had been around to keep her in line. Chloe hung the towel on the rack and walked into the gym. "Hey, Matt."

No answer.

She pulled one earpiece out. "How's it going?"

He shot her a glare. "Peachy."

Clearly, he wasn't as thrilled as Lindsay with Chloe's help. And though she didn't feel worthy to pray for herself, she offered a quick prayer on Matt's behalf. *Lord, please soften this boy and let me be Your instrument to help him.*

"I know this isn't much fun," she said, "but it probably beats going to juvie."

"I guess." He continued to roll yellow paint.

"Do you like sports?" Most guys liked to talk sports.

He shrugged. "I play some basketball."

Chloe pretended to inspect the paint job. "Mr. North wants to get some pickup basketball games going here when the center opens."

"Cool." Matt put finishing touches on the last spot and dropped the roller into the tray.

"Can you come into the games room for a minute? I want to show you the next area to paint."

Matt wiped his hands on a rag and, without a word, followed her across the floor.

"Obviously we want to brighten this room up," Chloe said as she flipped on the lights.

Matt snorted. "Yeah, this color stinks."

"It kinda does. So, what type of activities do you think we should do in here?"

His eyebrows rose to meet his bangs. "What do *I* think?"

"That's right. We're aiming for kids your age and up. So how about a Ping-Pong table? Maybe board games?"

He snorted again. "Board games? Try video

games."

"OK. Where would we get the equipment? We don't have a lot of money."

"Maybe someone could donate an older system."

"Good idea. What else would you like in here?"

"Air hockey. Maybe pinball."

"OK. I'll look into that."

"Really?" A hint of a smile hovered on Matt's face. "This place might not be so bad after all."

A surge of hope lifted Chloe's spirits. Matt needed a better group of friends to hang out with. Nick had practically bribed Maxi to befriend Chloe during her rebellious phase. She thanked God every day for the gift of Maxi's friendship and hoped she could find a positive influence for Matt.

Heavy footsteps thudded across the floor.

"Hey, Brown." A large, swarthy kid, who appeared older than Matt, stood in the doorway of the games room. He wore a dark bandana around his head, a black T-shirt, and baggy jeans with chains attached. Both his bottom lip and one eyebrow were pierced.

A chill ran down Chloe's arms at the hard look in their visitor's eyes.

"You finished here?" he asked Matt.

All the color bled from Matt's cheeks. "Not quite." He licked his lips, his gaze trained on the floor.

"I say you are. Come on, let's blow this place."

The guy's gaze moved to Chloe, as if in challenge.

She stiffened. "I'm sorry. No friends are allowed while Matt's working."

The boy moved closer, blocking the doorway and any chance of escape. "Who's going to make me leave?"

Chloe's authority seemed to have little effect. She chose to level him with a stare and folded her arms, more to stop her hands from shaking than to intimidate the kid.

He only laughed and took a menacing step forward.

Matt moved up beside her. "Hey, man. It's cool. I'll meet you later."

A tense silence followed. Uncomfortable vibes swirled in the air.

Chloe prayed he would leave. Perspiration broke out on her forehead, but she didn't dare wipe it away.

A loud squeak echoed through the gym as the main door opened.

Were more of Matt's 'friends' joining them? Muffled voices and a light laugh floated through to the games room.

The bully turned and stormed into the outer area.

"Hudson. What are you doing here?"

Chloe had never been more thankful to hear Dylan Moore's voice. She rushed into the gym with Matt close behind.

The guy stalked up to Lindsay and Dylan. "Just checking things out." He turned to glare at Matt. "See you later, Brown." A gust of wind blew in when the boy slammed out the front door.

Tension seeped from Chloe's body and she sagged against the gym wall.

Lindsay rushed over. "Are you all right, Miss Martin?"

"I'm fine. The fumes must be getting to me."

Dylan came to stand with Lindsay, a possessive hand on the girl's back.

Right now, Chloe could've kissed the boy. "Who

was that guy?" She pushed damp hair off her forehead.

"Jerry Hudson." Dylan sneered the name. "Head of one of the local gangs."

"He's a gang member?"

"Yeah. Not someone you want hanging around here."

Matt joined them. "Don't worry. I'll make sure he doesn't come back." Wariness shadowed his eyes.

Was Matt part of a gang? Chloe's spirits sank at the thought. No wonder Lindsay worried about him.

"I'll go clean the brushes, miss."

"Thank you, Matt. And thanks for your ideas. I'll pass them along to Mr. North."

"No prob."

"I'll give you a hand." Dylan followed Matt.

Chloe took some deep breaths, but the strong smell of paint didn't help her head.

"You sure you're OK?" Lindsay's face mirrored her concern.

"I'll be fine." Chloe forced her rubbery legs to move. "Let's keep Jerry Hudson's visit to ourselves. We don't need to give Mr. North a reason to worry."

Lindsay nodded, her eyes solemn. "I'm good at keeping secrets."

Chloe frowned as Lindsay went to join the boys. What other secrets was the girl hiding?

~*~

Aidan pulled into the lot of the rec center and jumped out of his car. He'd meant to drop by earlier to make sure Matt wasn't giving Chloe a hard time. As he jogged up the walkway, the main door swung open.

Lindsay, Dylan and Matt pushed outside.

"Hi, Mr. North," Lindsay said.

"Hi, guys. I was coming to check in with you, Matt. How's the painting going?"

"Good. Finished in the gym today. I'll start on the games room next."

"You've made excellent progress."

"Thanks." Matt pushed his hands into his hoodie pocket.

"We've got to get going," Lindsay said. "See you on Monday."

"Is Miss Martin still inside?"

Lindsay's pretty face creased into a frown. "Yes, but she wasn't feeling well."

Undercurrents of tension ran between the teens as they exchanged glances. What was that about?

"I'll go check on her. You kids have a good night."

"Thanks, Mr. North."

They scurried off as if given a reprieve.

Aidan pulled the main door open, noting it wasn't locked, and headed straight for the kitchen.

Chloe stood at the counter, packing some cleaning supplies into a bag.

"Hi, there."

She whirled around, hand to her throat. "Aidan. You scared me."

He took note of her pinched expression and the panic in her eyes. Something had her off-kilter. "Everything OK?"

"Fine. The kids just left." She fumbled for her purse with hands that trembled.

"Lindsay said you weren't feeling well."

"The paint fumes were making me dizzy. I'll be fine when I get some fresh air."

Why didn't he believe her? Maybe it was the way

she wouldn't meet his gaze. He chose not to challenge her. "Let's go then." Aidan picked up the bag of supplies, turned off the lights, and led her outside.

The night sky had taken on a pink glow, remnants of the recent sunset.

He locked up and handed her the keys. "I think you should keep the doors locked when you're here alone. You don't want any undesirables wandering in."

"Good idea." She leaned against her car, taking several deep breaths.

"Now that I think about it, I don't like the idea of you here alone with Matt. What if a bunch of his delinquent friends come in?"

Chloe bit her bottom lip, and looked away.

Alarm spiked his pulse. "Has that happened already?"

"One friend came by, but I told him he had to leave. It was no big deal."

Then why was she shaking? Whoever this kid was, he'd scared her. Aidan moved closer.

"From now on, somebody else needs to be with you. I'll come when I can, and when I'm not available, I'll get one of the other teachers to volunteer." His resistance wavered and he stroked a knuckle down her cheek. "I'm not taking any chances with your safety."

Relief washed over her features, although she said nothing. If it wasn't one of Matt's friends who scared her, then what had happened? She obviously didn't want to divulge anything. One thing Aidan couldn't tolerate was dishonesty and secrets, but until she was more comfortable with him, he wouldn't demand answers.

13

Lately the more time Chloe spent in Aidan's company, the more her feelings became harder to ignore. The possessive look in his eyes and the way he'd caressed her cheek left her rattled—and at the same time, thrilled. The fact that she *liked* that he cared about her enough to want to protect her—scared her more than Jerry Hudson's implied threats.

On her way home, the need for some sisterly advice led Chloe to Nick and Lily's house.

Mrs. Smythe, the new nanny, met her at the front door. "Good evening, Miss Chloe. Come in." The gray-haired woman in her lace-edged blouse and blue cardigan smiled.

While it felt odd to be invited into her family's house by a stranger, Chloe could not discount the value Mrs. Smythe added to her sister's home. Lily's health had improved, as had Nick's stress level, and the children adored her. Chloe had to admire the woman, who at triple her age, juggled all aspects of the Logan household without breaking a sweat.

"Thank you, Mrs. Smythe. Is Lily around?"

"She's in the living room. Mr. Nick is out at a meeting, and I'm afraid the girls are in bed."

Chloe followed her down the hallway.

"May I bring you a cup of tea?"

"That would be wonderful. Thank you."

Lily looked up from her book as Chloe entered the

room. "Chloe. What a nice surprise."

Chloe bent to kiss her sister's cheek. "Hope it's OK to drop by. I didn't feel like going home to an empty apartment."

Lily's shrewd eyes raked over her as Chloe dropped into one of the chairs near the fireplace. "Bad day?"

"You could say that." Chloe sighed. "Do you ever get the feeling you've bitten off more than you can chew?"

Lily chuckled, rubbing her belly. "You're kidding, right? Two babies and another on the way? Yeah, I can relate."

"Somehow I've gone from a chef in New York to teaching cooking in high school, mentoring a wayward teen, and trying to open my own shop. All in the space of a few weeks." *And fighting an attraction I didn't expect.*

"Do you think you could be trying to escape— filling your life with so many things that you don't have time to think about Richard?"

That's exactly what she was doing. Although lately another man occupied more of her thoughts.

"Don't you think it's time you told me what happened?" Lily's soft voice touched Chloe's pain. "You know you can tell me anything. That's what sisters are for."

Bone-weary fatigue left Chloe without her usual defenses. Wasn't this what she'd wished for growing up—a sister to share secrets with?

From the doorway, Mrs. Smythe cleared her throat. "Sorry to interrupt. I've brought your tea."

Lily waved her in. "Thank you, Clarissa. Please leave it on the table."

Mrs. Smythe set the tray down and left without a sound.

Chloe poured the tea into the delicate cups and handed one to Lily. The fire in the hearth bathed the area in a soothing glow. Everything about the room made Chloe feel safe. Maybe it was time. She needed to unburden her soul. Who better than her sister? She took a seat beside Lily on the couch.

"You seemed very much in love with Richard. So why did you break up?" Lily's gentle tone calmed Chloe's jagged nerves.

"I thought I loved him. At one point, I thought I couldn't live without him." She pushed aside memories of that dark place.

"He was a lot older than you, wasn't he?"

"That's what attracted me to him. He made me feel safe." Her voice caught. "I think I was looking for security. After Mama died, I felt so alone."

Lily's eyes shone with sympathy. "Nick and I were so busy being new parents...we didn't pay enough attention..."

"There wasn't anything you could do with me living in New York."

"So when the initial infatuation faded, you realized you weren't in love?"

"I wish it were that simple." Nick obviously hadn't told Lily that Richard was married. Chloe inhaled deeply and let it out slowly. "The truth is...Richard is married."

Lily's cup rattled in her saucer. "Oh, Chloe, no. He lied to you?"

How easy it would be to let Richard shoulder the entire blame. But it was time for her to take responsibility for her part in their sin.

She steeled herself for Lily's disappointment. "At first, yes. When I found out he was married, he swore he intended to leave his wife. He begged for more time. Said he couldn't live without me. I chose to believe he would leave when the time was right, and...I forgave him." She paused, the worst part still to come. "I continued the affair for months after I knew." Chloe dropped her face into her hands. "I don't think he ever intended to leave her." How clearly she could see his deception now. Why couldn't she see it then?

A warm arm came around her shoulders. "I'm so sorry, honey."

Chloe raised her eyes, blurred with moisture. "Don't you see? I'm just as guilty as Richard because I didn't end things. I went on in full knowledge of what I was doing to his wife and their children. What kind of person is willing to sacrifice a family's happiness for her own?" Tears spilled down her cheeks.

Lily dabbed a napkin to Chloe's face. "A very confused and lonely girl."

Chloe shook her head. "That's no excuse. Mama would be so ashamed of me. And Nick..." Her throat clogged with grief, imagining his disappointment in her.

"Shh. Let's not worry about Nick right now."

Chloe leaned against Lily's shoulder, drawing comfort from the warm solace she offered.

"What finally made you come home?"

Chloe straightened and wiped her face. Chills swept through her as she recalled that last horrible night. "Richard's wife found out about us. And she tried to kill me."

14

"Mr. North, there's a long distance call for you on line one." The school secretary's voice echoed into Aidan's office.

Four o'clock. After a week of helping Chloe supervise Matt at the youth center, Aidan knew Chloe and Matt would be there by now. He was running behind schedule, so he'd have to make this a fast call. "Thank you, Mrs. Grebbins." He picked up the phone. "Vice Principal North."

"Aidan. How are you?"

The female voice sent the blood rushing from Aidan's head. "Patricia? I'm fine. How are you?"

"I'm well, thanks. It's been a long time."

"It has. More than a year."

"You're probably surprised to hear from me." She sounded nervous.

Aidan's senses went on high alert. "What can I do for you?"

"I heard through the academic grapevine there might be a position open in your school. Is it true?"

His head spun as he mentally reviewed the staffing requirements. He wished he could lie and say there were no openings. But lying was one thing he could not abide—in anyone. "There's an upcoming maternity leave. Nothing permanent, why?"

"I'm thinking of making a change, and...Rainbow Falls sounds nice."

The blood in his veins turned frigid. He opened his mouth to speak, but no sound came out.

"Aidan, are you there?"

He cleared his throat. "I'm here. You just caught me off guard."

Her voice turned sultry. "In a good way, I hope."

"Frankly, Patricia, I don't think this position will suit you." He paused. "Why would you give up your seniority in Arizona to come out here? With no guaranteed long-term security?"

"I'm bored with everything here. The new principal and I don't see eye to eye."

Patricia must be doing her usual routine of creating drama for the new principal.

"Look, I'm not sure we should work together again."

"I thought you'd have forgiven me by now. But you're still mad, aren't you?"

He let out a sigh. "I'm not mad."

She sniffed. "I miss you, Aidan. I know I made a mistake, but I want another chance. We could start over fresh in Rainbow Falls, away from the gossip."

Her wheedling tone didn't soften his stance. "Not a good idea."

"Well, I guess that will depend on your principal. I'm coming for an interview next week."

He held back a groan. He did not need this aggravation right now.

"Think about what I said, Aidan. We'll talk when I'm there next week."

~*~

Chloe stopped in front of her shop and sent a text

message to Aidan to let him know she'd be back at the youth center as soon as possible. Of all times for a problem to crop up at the bakery—the one day Aidan was late to help supervise Matt.

She fit the key into the lock and pushed it open. Everything appeared exactly as she'd left it after she and Aidan had painted. A text message from a number she didn't recognize said there was a problem with the renovations. With an inspection pending, she couldn't take the chance that something might be wrong, like a burst pipe or some other catastrophe.

She locked the door and flipped the main light switch. The overhead lights did not come on. The interior remained shrouded in gloom, courtesy of the dark clouds threatening more rain. Had the power gone out during the last downpour? She swallowed a spurt of panic, remembering there was a flashlight under the counter. With a sigh of relief, she switched it on, and the bright beam illuminated the space.

When the light hit the wall, Chloe stifled a horrified cry. Violent slashes of red, still shiny and wet, marred the far wall. More vivid color dripped from the overturned wicker furniture. Anger, as deep and red as the splatters of paint, surged through her. Why would anyone do this?

She rushed back to the counter, and with shaking hands, rummaged through her purse for her cellphone. The police needed to know about this.

"I wouldn't do that if I were you."

She screamed and the phone slipped from her fingers.

Three male figures, hooded and masked, emerged from the shadows.

~*~

Aidan glanced at the clock and pressed his foot to the accelerator. He'd taken a few extra minutes to talk with Larry Jenkins about Patricia and was now half an hour late. He pulled into a parking spot closest to the front of the center and hurried inside. His gut burned. Probably shouldn't have had that third cup of coffee.

An eerie silence shrouded the empty gymnasium.

Where were Matt and Chloe?

Passing the dark kitchen, he entered the. games room.

Matt stood rolling paint onto the wall, headphones in place. The kid pulled out the earbuds when he noticed Aidan. "Hey, Mr. North."

"Hi, Matt. Nice job." Aidan admired the fresh coat of blue paint. "Where's Miss Martin?"

"She left a few minutes ago."

Aidan's neck muscles tightened. "To go where?"

"I'm not sure. She got a text message and had to leave."

Something urgent must have come up. Chloe wouldn't leave Matt alone unless it was important. When the phone in his pocket vibrated, he whipped it out, relieved to see a message from Chloe. Relief was short lived, however, when he read her cryptic note.

"Problem at the bakery. Back soon."

A prickle of unease chilled his spine. Something wasn't right. He had to find her.

~*~

Cold perspiration slid down Chloe's back. Fear froze her feet to the floor.

The hoodlums advanced, dark and menacing.

"What are you doing in here?" she demanded in her best 'teacher' voice. "This is private property."

The tallest one sneered and pulled his hand out.

The flashlight beam glinted off a steel blade. *He has a knife. Her* heart pounded a staccato refrain in her ears as she attempted to wet her bone-dry lips. "Who are you and what do you want?"

"First of all," said the apparent leader, "I want you to shut up. Second of all, we have a message for you."

Chloe locked her knees to keep them from shaking. If only her phone hadn't fallen back into her purse, she could speed dial someone. She glanced past the men. The door leading into the alley stood ajar, probably the way they'd broken in. If she ran, maybe she could make it outside. "What message?" She took two small steps forward.

"You need to stop interfering with a buddy of ours."

She forced herself to inhale slowly. "Who would that be?" Again she inched forward, almost clear of the counter.

"Matt Brown. Ever since you got involved, he's been less eager to spend time with us. Too busy painting."

The others cackled.

These must be Jerry's hoodlums, the ones influencing Matt to break the law.

"Matt's trying to stay out of jail. You can't blame him for that." Her shaking hands belied her brave words.

"No, but we can blame you." Hatred spilled from the eyes behind the mask.

It was now or never. She hurled the flashlight at the

closest thug, catching him in the temple. Amid their bellows of surprise, she burst across the room in a dead sprint.

Footsteps pounded the floor behind her.

Her breath heaved out in great gusts. Two more feet and she would reach the door.

One of them wrenched her back by the hair. Pain shot through her scalp, forcing a scream from her throat. Her feet left the ground, and she crashed to the cement floor near the alley door. As the villains advanced on her, she only had time for one final plea. *Please, God, don't let them kill me. I've got so much more to do.*

15

Chloe was in trouble. He could feel it.

Aidan's tires screeched when he came to an abrupt halt behind Chloe's car. The bakery's blank windows showed no sign of life. Why were the lights off? Knowing Chloe, every bulb should be blazing. He ran to the entrance and rattled the handle. Locked. "Chloe, are you in there?"

Furtive movements at the rear caused the hair to rise on his forearms. *Something wasn't right.* He raced down the side alley toward the back, hurdling fallen trashcans as he went, the smell of rotting garbage assaulting him.

Retreating footsteps echoed in the distance. Whoever it was had fled.

But where was Chloe?

His heart pumped a terrified beat. The back door stood wide open. "Chloe? Are you in here?" He pushed past overturned chairs and old paint cans, trying to find the light switch. Sweat slicked the back of his shirt to his skin.

A moan came from the corner of the room.

He rushed over, shoving debris out of the way.

Chloe lay sprawled on the floor, her legs twisted.

"Chloe!" He knelt beside her and brushed the hair off her face, flinching when his hand came away sticky. He could almost taste the metallic odor at the back of his throat. Panic curled in his stomach. *Please Lord, let her be all right.*

Aidan lifted her still form, carried her to his car, and laid her on the seat. Under the car light, she looked ethereal, her skin devoid of all color. Blood ran from her temple and soaked the front of her shirt.

With unsteady hands, he moved her hair aside and felt for the wound. A gash above her ear oozed blood. "Chloe, can you hear me?" He pulled a hanky from his jacket and pressed it against the cut. With his other hand, he caressed her pale face.

Long lashes fanned out onto her cheeks.

"Wake up, honey. Please."

A small groan escaped her lips as her eyelids fluttered, and then flew open. Terror filled the amber depths. "Aidan." She leapt up and buried her face in his neck. "Are they gone?"

"Yes. You're safe now."

Huge tremors wracked her frame.

He gathered her onto his lap and stroked her back, murmuring soothing words. "We have to get you to the doctor," he said at last.

She swiped away her tears. "What about my shop? We need to call the police."

"I'll call Chief Hillier. Meanwhile I'm taking you to get checked out." Should he take her to the hospital in Kingsville or let Doc Anderson handle it? He pulled out his phone and called the doctor's office.

When he explained the situation, Doc told him to bring Chloe right over.

Aidan then dialed the police and left a message with the receptionist, who assured him she'd get the chief right over. He turned his attention back to Chloe as he started the engine.

"They sprayed red paint everywhere. Why would

they do that?" she whispered.

He hadn't even thought to check out the main area of the shop. "Do you know who they were?"

A solitary tear escaped her lashes.

She shuddered and he mentally cursed his insensitivity. "Never mind. We'll talk about it later."

~*~

Chloe's head throbbed. Her limbs shook and her insides trembled. Whenever she closed her eyes, visions of the masked hoodlums forced them open again. Despite her discomfort, she attempted to focus her thoughts.

Aidan had asked whether she knew her assailants.

If she implicated friends of Matt's, she might create a lot more trouble for the boy. Should she say anything or feign ignorance?

Aidan stopped the car in front of Doc Anderson's medical clinic.

A sudden thought struck her as Aidan helped her out of the car. What if the villains went to the youth center to continue their reign of terror on Matt? She gripped Aidan's sleeve. "Did you leave Matt alone?"

"I asked Nick to go over and stay with him."

A cry of protest stuck in her throat. Nick could be in the line of fire too. The steely glint of the knife blade flashed through her mind. She clutched tighter. "Call him. Make sure they're OK."

"As soon as you've seen the doctor."

"No. Now."

Aidan's gray eyes darkened to charcoal. "What aren't you telling me, Chloe?"

Her legs almost buckled. Only Aidan's grip kept

her upright. Though still hesitant to reveal that Matt was involved with probable gang members, the very real physical danger seemed more urgent. "The guys who attacked me knew Matt. What if they went after him when they left my shop?"

A frown creased Aidan's forehead. "I'll call as soon as we get you inside."

Doc Anderson immediately beckoned them in. He shooed Aidan into the waiting area, and then ushered Chloe into the examining room. "That's a nasty looking gash, young lady. Care to tell me what happened?"

Chloe gave him a brief explanation. She gritted her teeth while Doc cleaned and treated her head wound.

He ruled out a concussion, said she didn't need stitches, and told her the headache might last a day or two. Other than that, he pronounced her fit.

Chloe swallowed the pain tablets he gave her and stepped out of the examining room.

Aidan jumped to his feet. "How is she?" he asked the doctor.

Doc laid a reassuring hand on Chloe's shoulder. "It wasn't as bad as it looked. Head wounds always bleed a lot. Still, she's very fortunate. A few inches over and that blow might have been a whole lot more serious." He peered at her. "You take it easy tomorrow, young lady. Get lots of rest, and put some ice on that bump."

"I will. Thanks, Doc." As soon as they stepped outside, Chloe turned to Aidan. "Did you talk to Nick?"

"Yes. They're both fine. Nick took Matt home."

"Thank God."

Aidan's eyes narrowed. "I have some questions for you once I get you home." His phone went off just as they reached the car. "Hey, Mike." He listened for a moment then looked at Chloe. "Let me ask her. Are you up to talking with Chief Hillier now? If not, we can do it tomorrow."

"Ask him if he'll come to the apartment. I can't go back to the shop right now."

~*~

Chloe leaned against the back of her couch and relished the coldness of the icepack on her head. The interview with Chief Hillier had been draining. She hated having to admit that the thugs were connected to Matt, not wishing to cause him more problems.

The chief left with the promise to drive by the Browns' apartment to make sure no unsavory characters were hanging around.

"This was all my fault." Aidan's gruff voice jarred Chloe's eyes open. He stood by the fireplace, his back stiff.

"How was it your fault?"

"If I hadn't been late getting to the youth center..." A nerve ticked in his jaw.

"It wouldn't have made any difference, Aidan."

He turned fiery eyes on her. "I would've taken one look at that bogus message and either gone with you, or had Mike check it out instead." Aidan paced the length of the living room, running his hands through his dark hair. He'd rolled the sleeves of his dress shirt up to his elbows and loosened his tie. The whole disheveled appearance endeared him to her even more.

"I'm so sorry," she said. "For being taken in by a phony text message, and for not telling you who the thugs were right away."

Aidan's features softened, and he returned to sit beside her. "No. I'm the one who's sorry. I shouldn't be taking my frustration out on you." He took one of her hands. "You have no idea what I went through finding you like that."

She squeezed his fingers, a lump rising in her throat. "I never got the chance to thank you for coming when you did. If you hadn't been there to scare them off…" Visions of the masked man holding a knife on her made her mouth go dry. "When they heard you at the door, they panicked and hit me over the head."

"Oh, that makes me feel better," he said wryly.

"They were going to cut my face." A shudder went through her.

He stared intently into her eyes and cupped her cheek with his palm. "I'm very happy they didn't get the chance."

Chloe forgot to breathe as a hum of electricity passed through her body. She leaned further into his hand, seeking the comfort he offered—and so much more. "How did you know to come?" she whispered.

"I don't know—I just did."

Their gazes locked and held.

Her breathing became shallow. The intoxicating smell of his cologne mixed with his unique masculine scent, filling her senses as her lids fluttered closed.

His lips met hers in a quick brush and then retreated—a sweet tease to torment her, making her want so much more. She trembled as she waited and hoped.

Aidan let out a low groan and pulled her tight against him, crushing his mouth to hers.

The feel of his lips on hers ignited something deep within her, making her pulse race. An intense rush of emotion filled her as she kissed him back.

"Aidan," she whispered.

A storm of torment crossed his face. He rested his forehead against hers, his breathing ragged. "I promised myself we wouldn't do this again." He sighed and scrubbed a hand over his face. "But the thought of what could have happened tonight..." Regret darkened his eyes as he picked up the forgotten ice pack and held it out. "You should get some rest. Keep the ice on a while longer."

She nodded, her system still reeling. "Aidan?"

"Yes?"

"Would you stay until I fall asleep?" She just couldn't bear to be alone yet.

"Sure."

"Thank you." She laid her head on one of the pillows.

Aidan draped a knitted blanket over her. "I'll put another log on the fire so it'll stay warm in here."

She sighed. The more Chloe was around Aidan, the more she admired him. He reminded her so much of Nick—and of her late father—a good, kind, and dependable man. She closed her eyes, but Aidan's face filled her mind. She was sorry he felt their kiss was a mistake. Because this time she couldn't regret it.

16

Aidan stared at the blank computer screen after closing an e-mail from Mrs. Merriweather. Due to complications, she would require more time to heal. Which meant Chloe would be helping at the school for longer than the few weeks he'd anticipated. He swallowed a gulp of cold coffee and grimaced.

This new development reinforced the need to put the brakes on their growing relationship. No more passionate kisses. His pulse tripped just thinking about it. But it wouldn't look good to have a romantic relationship with one of the school volunteers.

Mr. Jenkins had made his policy on such matters very clear, and Aidan couldn't afford another black mark—not after the fiasco in Arizona. He pushed up from his chair, shoved his fists into his pockets and walked to the window. At that terrifying moment when he'd found Chloe unconscious and thought he'd lost her, the truth had hit him like a swift punch to the gut. He was falling in love with her—and he had no idea what to do about it.

A rap at his door brought his attention back to the present. It couldn't be Chloe. She would be in the kitchen with the students. Though he'd tried to get her to take the day off, she'd insisted on coming in.

The door swung inward.

Aidan froze. "Patricia." How had he forgotten she was coming for an interview today?

She was as lovely as ever, her shoulder-length blonde hair perfectly groomed. "Hello, Aidan. It's good to see you." She moved forward to embrace him and the familiar scent of her expensive perfume surrounded him.

He stepped behind the safety of his desk. "Please have a seat."

She pouted brightly painted lips and sat in the guest chair.

"Have you finished your interview?" Aidan couldn't help but compare Patricia's artfully enhanced good looks to Chloe's natural beauty.

"Yes. I'm on my way out, but I couldn't leave without seeing you." She smiled at him. "I wanted to see if you were free for dinner. My plane doesn't leave until eight."

Aidan stiffened. "I'm sorry, Patricia. I don't think that's a good idea."

The pain of her betrayal came thudding back, churning his stomach. He stood, forcing her to follow suit, and checked his watch. "If you'll excuse me, I have to be somewhere in fifteen minutes. Have a nice trip back."

He prayed she didn't get the position. Her constant presence here would be unbearable. Maybe he'd have another talk with Larry before he made his final decision. The man had a right to know about their past connection and possible conflict of interest. Aidan headed toward the door.

Patricia followed and laid a hand on his arm. "You'll never know how sorry I am about the way I handled things with you." Actual tears appeared at the corners of her blue eyes.

He wanted to say, "I forgive you." But the words

wouldn't come. Instead he said, "What's done is done. Let's forget it."

"I was hoping you'd say that."

Before he could move, she planted her lips on his. Shock slammed through him, and his whole body went rigid. Scowling, he gripped her upper arms and set her away from him. The heated words he intended to say froze in his throat as a movement over Patricia's shoulder caught his attention.

Chloe stood staring at him, open-mouthed, in the doorway. "Excuse me. I'll come back later." She pulled the door shut with a sharp click. Her retreating footsteps echoed down the tiled hallway.

Aidan had a sinking feeling that his life was about to become very complicated.

~*~

Chloe rubbed her temples, trying to ease the throbbing headache—a souvenir of yesterday's assault. She'd managed to get Matt to the youth center early and needed him to finish up so she could leave before Aidan arrived. She couldn't cope with another confrontation after what she'd witnessed in his office. An uncomfortable flare of jealousy twisted her stomach muscles. The image of Aidan kissing that sleek blonde had shaken her almost as much as the attack in the bakery. How could he share such a passionate kiss with her last night, and then embrace some other woman today?

"Miss Martin? I'm finished." Matt stood in the kitchen doorway, hands tucked in his jean pockets.

Despite the headache, she needed to talk to him about what had happened. "Matt, has Chief Hillier called you today?"

A frown formed under his shaggy bangs. "No. Why?"

"Something happened yesterday at my shop." She took a breath. "Three men broke in, vandalized the place, and…" she swallowed, "and hit me." She touched tentative fingers to the still-tender area above her ear.

His eyes widened. "I'm sorry, miss. Are you OK?"

"I'm fine. I don't want you to feel bad, but I think they were friends of yours. They warned me to leave you alone."

His jaw hardened to match his eyes. "They're no friends of mine."

"Who are they then?"

His mouth tightened, but he said nothing.

She took a tentative step toward him. "We had to report the incident to the police, so Chief Hillier will probably want to talk to you. I'm so sorry, Matt. Is there anything I can do?"

"No. I'll handle it." He turned and stormed across the gym.

Chloe grabbed her bag, hurried to the outer door, and locked up. She turned around, dismayed to find Matt hadn't waited for her. Now she'd have to go looking for him.

Chloe jumped at the sound of a car pulling into the lot. Visions of the masked men from yesterday exploded through her mind. Her breathing went shallow as she turned.

Aidan slammed out of his car and crossed the walkway.

Her initial relief faded, and a new tension took its place.

He ripped off his sunglasses as he approached. "Chloe, we need to talk."

"Not now, Aidan. Matt has run off, and I need to find him."

"What happened?" Concern shadowed his eyes.

"I told him about the vandals. He got upset and ran off." She threw out her hands in despair. "I'm afraid he'll do something stupid."

He shoved his glasses back on. "Come on. I'll help you look for him."

~*~

Aidan rammed the gearshift into drive and pulled away from the curb outside the Browns' apartment. Everywhere they'd searched had turned up empty. Matt was nowhere to be found, and he wasn't answering his phone. *Please, Lord, don't let him get in any more trouble. Watch over him and keep him safe.* Aidan glanced at Chloe.

She sat in the passenger seat, her head back, eyes closed.

"Headache still bad?"

She nodded and rubbed a hand across her forehead.

"Matt will turn up. Don't worry." He reached over to squeeze her hand, but she flinched and pulled away. Aidan inhaled, shocked at how much that tiny gesture could hurt. His thoughts circled back to the reason he'd wanted to see her. "About earlier today—what you saw in my office wasn't what it seemed."

She stiffened. "You don't owe me any explanation."

Unexpected anger surfaced. He pulled the car into

an empty lot to give her his full attention. "How can you say that after what we shared last night?" He regretted his harsh tone when hurt bloomed in her eyes. In a softer voice, he continued. "I'm not the kind of man who would kiss you one day and someone else the next. I hope you know that."

She didn't answer, only clutched the locket around her neck.

Aidan fought an insane urge to pull her into his arms and kiss her until all disbelief had evaporated. Instead he focused on the passing traffic. "Patricia is my ex-girlfriend. She was here for an interview and dropped by to say hello. I was showing her out when she ambushed me with that kiss."

Chloe seared him with a heated look. "Is it a coincidence she came all the way from Arizona to apply for a job here?"

"No. She's made it clear she wants me back." He gripped the steering wheel. "But that'll never happen."

"Why did you break up?"

Maybe if he opened up to her about his failed relationship, she'd confide in him about her own painful past. "We worked at a private Christian school where every teacher was held to exacting standards of behavior. Dating among the teachers was discouraged, so Patricia and I kept our relationship quiet. After a while, she started hinting at an engagement ring. I was not ready for that, but she ignored my wishes and told everyone we were getting engaged. She hinted at…" He paused, fighting the rise of heat, "at an intimate relationship. Word got around to the principal. I'm not sure he ever believed it wasn't true."

"She sounds desperate."

"When the incident with my student happened,

the ugly rumors became too much for her, and she walked away. Not long after, the principal asked me to leave." He shifted his gaze to the windshield, not daring to look at Chloe.

"If she loved you, she would've stood by you." Warm sympathy oozed from her voice.

"That's how I felt. Totally betrayed by the one person who should have been on my side." He relaxed his grip on the steering wheel.

"I'm sorry I jumped to the wrong conclusion and didn't give you a chance to explain."

The boulder of tension rolled off his shoulders. "It must have looked really bad. I can imagine how I'd feel in the same position."

"How *would* you feel, Aidan?"

Shivers went down his spine. It was much too soon to verbalize his feelings, as convoluted as they were. Yet the vulnerability on her face tore at him. "I care about you very much, Chloe. More than I ever expected—"

Her cellphone went off. She gave an apologetic shrug. "It might be about Matt." Seconds later, her expectant expression morphed into a frown. "What do you want, Richard?"

Aidan's shoulders stiffened.

She listened intently. "I'm sorry. How's Denise?" A variety of emotions flickered across her expressive face. "I'm sorry for your loss, but this doesn't change anything. Please don't call me again." She disconnected and squeezed her eyes shut.

"Is everything all right?"

She opened her eyes and nodded.

"What did he want?"

"This isn't the time to get into it."

Slivers of suspicion rippled under his skin. "I just told you the sordid details of my relationship. Now it's your turn." She needed to trust him enough to reveal her secrets.

"I'm sorry. I—I can't right now."

The thin thread holding his patience together evaporated. "Who is Denise, Chloe? And what does she have to do with Richard?"

The color bled out of Chloe's cheeks, leaving them ashen. "Denise is Richard's wife."

17

This was not the way Chloe had planned to tell Aidan about Richard's marital status.

"He's married?"

"Yes."

Aidan slammed a fist on the dashboard. "That low-life." He shot her a hard look, his brows forming an ominous line. "What did you do when you found out?"

She hesitated, totally unprepared for this conversation. Aidan would hate her if she told him the truth. Needing air, Chloe pushed out the door. She gulped in several deep breaths, trying to ease the pounding in her temples.

Aidan's tall frame blocked the sunlight. "Tell me you broke up with the jerk."

"I broke up with him." She just didn't mention when.

"You must have been furious when you found out."

Horrid memories of that day swamped her. The anger, the crying, the shouting. She never wanted to experience that type of emotional turmoil again. "I was devastated."

"How did you handle it?"

"Not well." Panic inched across her nerve endings. Her cellphone rang, and she dug it out, not even caring if it was Richard again. Anything to avoid Aidan's probing.

"Chloe. It's Nick." His voice sounded grim. "We're on the way to the hospital. Lily's in labor."

~*~

Aidan frowned. Something had upset Chloe again. Her face had drained of color.

"All right. I'll meet you there." She charged back toward the car, phone to her ear. "Tell Lily I love her."

"Chloe, what is it?"

She yanked open the passenger door. "Can you take me to my car, please? Lily's in labor. I need to get to the hospital."

He headed to the driver's side. "I'll take you."

"That's not necessary." She slammed the door shut.

No way was he letting her drive in this emotional state. She'd be a car accident waiting to happen. "We're closer to Kingsville here. If we go back for your car, you'll add an extra half hour to the trip."

She seemed to wrestle with his logic, her hands shaking. "But it could be hours until the baby's born."

He pulled out of the lot. "I can wait with you. I've got nothing on for tonight."

"What about Matt? Someone needs to make sure he's not in trouble."

"I'll have Mike look for him."

Chloe laid her head back. "Fine. Let's go."

The forty-mile drive to the Kingsville Hospital went by in a blur. Aidan called Mike, filled him in on Matt's last whereabouts and the problem of his disappearance. Mike promised to look for the teen.

Aidan's mind reeled from the implications of

Chloe's confession. No wonder Chloe was leery of men. No wonder she'd turned tail and run at the sight of him kissing a strange woman in his office. A thousand questions swirled, but for now he put them on hold. When things settled down, Aidan planned to have a serious talk with her.

They reached the hospital in record time and found the maternity ward on the second floor.

Chloe inquired about Lily at the nursing station.

"If you'll wait here, I'll check on the patient's progress." A stout, older woman, whose nametag said Matilda, pointed them to a waiting area across the way.

Chloe remained in the hallway, arms folded, staring after the retreating woman.

Aidan laid a hand on her shoulder. "Come on. Let's sit down. She'll be back soon." He guided her into the room. "Are you hungry? I could get you something from the cafeteria."

"No, thanks. I couldn't eat right now."

"A drink, then?"

She shook her head.

His own stomach rumbled, but he would wait. He led her to a bank of seats. "Lily's in good hands. I'm sure the baby will be fine."

"I'm scared for her, Aidan. What if her blood pressure goes up during labor? It's been better lately, but—"

He took one of her hands. Her fingers were cold, rigid with tension. With slow strokes, he massaged them until he felt the blood returning, hoping his warmth would infuse her with calmness.

She leaned her head against his shoulder and gave a light sigh. "Did you know Maxi and Jason delivered

Annabelle at home?"

He chuckled. "I'd forgotten about that. Maxi was pretty freaked out when she called me the next day."

"I'm just glad Lily's in a hospital now."

Matilda poked her head in the room. "Miss North, you can see your sister now. I'll show you to her room."

Chloe bolted up. "Thank you." She turned back to Aidan. "Will you wait for me?"

His heart turned over at the vulnerability shining in her wide eyes, and he nodded. "I'm not going anywhere."

~*~

Chloe peeked into the delivery room, nerves making her legs unsteady. The antiseptic smell of hospitals gave her the creeps. Attached to Lily's bed, a bevy of machines hummed and beeped. That couldn't be a good sign.

"Chloe. Come on in." Nick stood at the side of the bed where Lily lay with her eyes closed. "She's resting for a bit. The contractions have been intense."

Chloe stepped into Nick's arms for a hug. Haggard lines of worry etched his face. "What did the doctor say?"

"They're keeping a close watch on her blood pressure and if it gets too high, they may have to do an emergency Caesarean."

"Maybe that would be best."

"I think so too, but Lily doesn't want a Caesarean."

Lily gave a slight moan and opened her eyes.

Chloe stepped toward her, and Lily gripped her

outstretched hand with the strength of three men.

"Thanks for coming." Her face crumpled in a grimace. "Sorry—another contraction." She began breathing hard, almost panting.

"That's right, honey. You're doing great," Nick encouraged.

Lily slumped back against the pillow. Sweat glued her hair to her damp face.

Nick spooned some ice chips into her mouth.

Chloe continued to stroke Lily's arm, offering comfort.

Another pain gripped Lily. She stiffened and clenched Chloe's hand so hard that Chloe thought her fingers might crack. The breathing didn't seem to work this time. A scream burst from Lily's throat.

Fear pooled in Chloe's stomach, becoming a roll of nausea. "Help her."

Nick seemed just as fearful.

The machines began to beep at an alarming rate.

A doctor and two nurses rushed in. "Out of the way please." They fussed around Lily's bed, working quickly. The man in blue scrubs turned to them. "We're taking her to the OR. You two will have to stay here. We'll let you know when it's over."

Nick gripped the metal rail of Lily's bed. "I'm going with her."

The doctor's voice softened somewhat. "I'm sorry, son. Not in this type of emergency situation."

Nick nodded, but tears moistened his eyes. He bent to kiss Lily's forehead. "I'll be right outside, honey, and I'll be praying."

~*~

Aidan tried to read a magazine. He threw it aside, jumped up and paced back and forth until he'd memorized the pattern of the tiles. What if this was his baby? What would he be like then? The idea gave him pause. He'd never given serious thought to having children, yet now his mind conjured up Chloe as a mother. *Where had that idea come from?*

He looked up to see Chloe rushing down the hall, a hand clutched to her mouth.

Aidan's stomach twisted with dread. Something must be wrong.

When she saw him, she threw herself into his arms. "Oh, Aidan."

His heart jerked hard, but he waited until she calmed down.

"They took Lily for an emergency Caesarean. The doctor looked worried."

"Let's get Nick and go to the chapel," he said gently.

But Nick didn't want to be too far away in case he missed the doctor.

So the three sat in the waiting area and prayed for the safety of Lily and the baby. Nick and Chloe seemed considerably calmer when they'd finished. They sat in silence, hands joined, and waited.

Aidan's heart swelled with tenderness when Chloe's head drooped once more against his shoulder. If Nick wasn't there, he'd have pulled her closer.

After an eternity of waiting, the doctor entered the room. "Congratulations, Mr. Logan. You have a son."

Nick shot to his feet. "Is my wife OK?"

"She's doing well. If you'd like to hold your son, they're cleaning him up in the nursery."

Nick blinked, and then stared down the hall. "I

don't want to leave in case Lily needs me..." The indecision on his face was heart-wrenching.

Chloe laid her hand on Nick's arm, smiling through her tears. "Go on. If there's any word, I'll come and get you."

Nick hesitated a moment more, then gave Chloe a kiss, and hurried down the hall.

Aidan pulled Chloe into a light hug.

"I have a nephew." She smiled. "Can we pray some more? I want to thank God for getting Lily through this and for blessing our family."

18

Cocooned on the couch in her apartment, Chloe thanked God again for the safe arrival of little David Nicholas. Despite being early, the baby weighed six pounds and, according to Nick, possessed a well-developed set of lungs. By the time Chloe laid eyes on her new nephew, he'd been sound asleep, a tiny angel in his father's arms.

Although weak, Lily's blood pressure had leveled off right after the delivery and she was recovering nicely. A relieved Nick wouldn't budge from her side for a second. Aidan and Chloe had brought him some food and coffee, and then left the couple alone.

By the time they got back to Rainbow Falls, Chloe had realized she was starving, and Aidan offered to do a food run.

The door to Chloe's apartment swung open.

Aidan entered with takeout bags from the Chinese restaurant. "Hope you like fried rice and chicken balls."

"Perfect. Thanks for getting the food. My fridge is unusually bare these days."

Aidan grinned. "Mine's not much better." He set the food on the coffee table, handed her a soda, and took a seat beside her on the couch.

She studied his handsome features as he opened the containers. He had steadied her tonight. She never would have made it through those scary few hours without his calming presence at her side, praying with her. Aidan North was a man she could count on in times of crisis. "Thank you for staying at the hospital with me."

"There's nowhere else I would've been."

"Praying together was wonderful. I haven't felt so close to God in a long time. Even though I have no right to—" She broke off, fearful she'd ruined the moment.

Aidan's chopsticks stilled. "Everyone has a right to talk to God, Chloe. No matter what."

"Do you think God forgives everything, Aidan? Even the worst sins?"

"Yes, I do. There's nothing so terrible that God won't forgive. Most times we're the ones who can't forgive ourselves."

"You're right. Every time I think about Richard's wife and kids, I don't think I can ever forgive myself."

A muscle in his jaw ticked. "It wasn't your fault. The blame lies squarely with that jerk for misleading you."

Here was the perfect opportunity to tell Aidan the complete truth—that she didn't break up with Richard right away but continued their illicit liaison for months afterward. But Chloe couldn't bring herself to risk breaking the close bond they had forged tonight.

Aidan set his container aside and picked up his cellphone. "I'd better call Mike. He left a message earlier."

She exhaled, ashamed at the relief that swept over her.

"Hey, Mike. Sorry to call so late. We just came from the hospital. Lily and Nick have a son." He chuckled at Mike's response. "I know. So any news on

Matt?"

Chloe straightened. *If I can ask for one more favor, Lord, please let Matt be safe.*

"I see. Thanks. I'll talk to you tomorrow."

She finished her food while he put his phone away. "Well?"

"Mike found Matt near the school. He'd been roughed up a bit, but he's OK."

Chloe gasped. "How roughed up?"

"A bloody nose and probably a black eye by tomorrow. But he's fine. Wouldn't tell Mike a thing though."

"Still protecting those gangsters."

Aidan's eyes narrowed. "Gangsters?"

"Dylan Moore told me one of them might be in a gang. The ones who vandalized my shop sure seemed like gang members." She shivered at the memory of the masked men.

"That would explain Matt's odd behavior. It'll be almost impossible to get him out of a gang if he's been initiated."

"Have you ever spoken with Matt's mother?"

"No. She's never returned my calls. Lindsay keeps running interference for her."

The niggling fear that had bothered Chloe for a while now resurfaced. "What if there's no mother living there? Or she's incapacitated in some way?"

Aidan wiped his hands on a napkin. "I'd be forced to call County Social Services and report neglect. They'd probably put Matt into foster care. Maybe Lindsay, as well."

Chloe's spirits sank. Having an absentee parent was less than ideal, yet it had to be better than the foster care system.

"I was thinking," Aidan said, "since Matt is almost finished at the youth center, maybe he could continue his community work at your shop."

"That's a great idea." She stuffed all the garbage into one bag.

"When are you planning to open?"

"I was hoping for the beginning of December, in time for the Christmas rush. Why?"

"Mrs. Merriweather's injury isn't healing as well as the doctors hoped." He raised his gaze to hers. "Which leads me to ask, how long can you continue assisting her?"

"Once the bakery opens, I won't have time for both. Can you find someone else by then?"

"I guess I'll have to. You've already stayed longer than anticipated."

"Well, I enjoy it. The kids are great."

"And all the boys have a crush on the teacher's aide." His eyes twinkled. "Can't say I blame them." Aidan slid closer on the couch.

Heat from his body hit her in a wave. He raised a hand to brush a strand of hair off her face, creating tingles down her spine in anticipation of his kiss.

But at the last minute, he pulled away and cleared his throat.

Her body balked at the sudden absence of his warmth, adding to the disappointment that flooded her system.

Aidan gave a soft chuckle. "You are much too tempting for your own good, Miss Martin." He tipped her chin up with one finger. "I'm giving you fair warning that come December, when you're no longer at the school, I'll be pulling out the old North charm. You won't be able to resist."

"We'll see about that." Chloe laughed.

Yet deep down, she knew he was right. She didn't stand a chance.

~*~

At the end of class the next morning, Chloe caught Lindsay before she left the kitchen. "How is Matt? Is he badly hurt?"

"He'll be OK." The girl didn't look well herself. All the color had left her face, and dark circles made her eyes seem hollow.

Chloe lowered her voice. "Lindsay, I have to ask. Is Matt involved in a gang?"

"I-I can't talk now. I have to meet Dylan." Lindsay avoided eye contact as she untied her apron.

"Please know you can talk to me about anything. I mean it. I'll do whatever I can to help."

Lindsay gave a quick nod, and then ran out the door.

Chloe heaved a sigh. The girl was hiding something big. Chloe could feel it. She had to get Lindsay to open up. Maybe a private setting would help. With that in mind, Chloe waited for Lindsay in the school parking lot after the final bell.

Lindsay and Dylan came out the main doors together, looking anything but happy. They seemed to be arguing as they made their way through the parked vehicles. Dylan's face wore a dark scowl. Lindsay stood with her arms wrapped around her as if to shield herself.

Chloe moved closer, prepared to jump in if necessary.

Dylan stalked to a sporty-looking car, flung the

door open, and jumped in. He started the engine and gunned out of the spot.

Lindsay's shoulders slumped as he sped away.

Chloe waited a few seconds, and then approached cautiously. "Lindsay? Is everything OK?"

The girl whirled around, tears streaking her pale face. Freckles stood out against the pallor, making her appear much younger than seventeen.

"Did you and Dylan have a fight?"

"Y—yes."

As much as Chloe had hoped that the two would break up, she hated the misery on Lindsay's face. "Come on. I'll drive you home."

The girl nodded and followed Chloe to her car.

"Do you want to get a soda and talk?" Chloe asked as they pulled out of the lot.

"No, thanks. I just want to go home."

"Care to tell me what's wrong?"

"No." Lindsay stared out the window.

Don't push it, Chloe. Maybe she's not ready to open up.

Two blocks from her home, Lindsay stiffened. "Stop the car." She clasped one hand over her mouth, the other over her stomach.

Chloe pulled into a gas station. Before she could shift into park, Lindsay dashed out of the car. Seconds later, she retched on the grass by the sidewalk.

Concern shot through Chloe. She fished a tissue out of her purse. Gently she held the girl's hair until she had finished, and then wiped her face.

"Thanks."

"You're welcome. Go wait in the car and I'll get some water."

When Chloe returned, a bit of color had come back into Lindsay's cheeks. "Feeling better?" Chloe twisted the lid off the water bottle and handed it to her.

"Yes, thanks." Lindsay took a long swallow.

"Are you sick, honey?" Chloe held her breath.

Lindsay shook her head. Tears bloomed in her eyes.

"Do you want to tell me what's going on?" Chloe kept her voice gentle. If ever this girl needed someone, it was now.

Moisture slid down her cheeks. "I think I might be pregnant."

19

Aidan paced his living room in an attempt to expel his pent up frustration. He'd left school early today—in time to witness Chloe leaving the parking lot with Lindsay Brown.

His repeated warnings about the risk of getting involved with her students seemed to fall on deaf ears. What could he do to get through to her?

He snatched his phone and started to punch in a heated text message. The device rang in his hand before he could finish. "Chloe?"

"No, it's Nick."

"Oh, hey." Aidan forced his mind in a different direction. "How are Lily and the baby?"

"Lily's tired and sore but doing well. And little Davey's perfect."

"I'm glad. So what can I do for you?"

"I'm home to have dinner with the girls and grab a shower. But I was wondering if you could come by before I head back to the hospital. Say around seven?"

"I guess so." Apprehension shot through Aidan at the unusual request.

"Good. See you then."

~*~

Nick answered the door and ushered Aidan into the living room. The lines around Nick's eyes told of his exhaustion.

"First of all, thank you for bringing Chloe to the hospital last night. And thanks for staying. Having you guys there made all the difference."

"Glad I could help."

Nick leaned against the mantel. Light from the fireplace danced across his rugged features. "I'm curious though. Why were you and Chloe together when I called?"

His casual tone didn't fool Aidan. He'd heard it often enough. "We were looking for a missing student."

"I see."

Unease churned in Aidan's stomach. "What's this about, Nick?"

Nick took a seat across from Aidan. "We've been friends long enough that I hope I can be frank."

"Of course."

"You've been spending a lot of time with Chloe lately. I've seen the way you look at her, and I recognize that look, because I had the same one the moment I met Lily."

"I don't—"

Nick held up a hand. "Let me finish."

A bead of sweat snaked down Aidan's spine.

"Chloe's in a vulnerable place right now," Nick went on. "I don't know if she's told you about her recent breakup?"

Aidan rose and stalked across the room. "She told me yesterday that her ex was married."

"Yeah." Grim lines bracketed Nick's mouth. "I may be a minister, but I'd like to get my hands around that guy's throat for one second."

"You and me both." Aidan shoved his clenched

fists deep into his pockets.

"My point is, I don't think Chloe's emotionally ready for another relationship right now. And I don't want to see her hurt again."

Tension like a taut wire banded across Aidan's shoulders. "Are you asking me to stay away from her?"

Nick narrowed the gap between them. Blue intensity spilled from his eyes. "Yes. Give her some space to get over this...mess before she acts impulsively on the rebound. I'm thinking of *your* welfare here too."

Aidan ran his hands over his jaw. A seesaw of emotions warred in his mind. Nick wasn't saying anything Aidan hadn't already told himself. "I'll agree for now—while she's working at the school. After that, I can't make any promises."

Nick's scowl deepened. "Not good enough."

Aidan understood Nick's objection wasn't personal, only a misguided attempt at protection. "Did you listen when people warned you to stay away from Lily?"

Nick jerked visibly, a nerve ticking in his jaw. "No."

"Then have a little faith. The last thing I would do is hurt Chloe."

Nick finally nodded, looking far from satisfied.

Aidan smiled. "Hey, you're the minister. Why not trust God to handle this for you?"

Nick gave a weary smile, lightening the tension between them. "Guess prayer is my only option for now. Short of locking Chloe in my attic for the next year."

"Good luck with that, my friend. Not even an attic

would stop Hurricane Chloe."

~*~

Chloe handed the newly-purchased pregnancy test to Lindsay in the teen's messy bedroom. "Here you go. I'll be in the kitchen if you need me."

Chloe headed back through the living room. She surveyed the cluttered area and itched to scrub the place down. In the kitchen, she found a garbage bag, and began to clear away empty pizza boxes and soda cans, trying not to cringe at the evidence of mice droppings. She stacked dirty dishes on the counter and washed the small table. Anything to keep her hands busy so she didn't chew her nails.

Five minutes turned to ten.

Unable to contain her impatience, Chloe knocked on the bathroom door. "Lindsay? You OK?"

No response.

"Do you need more time?"

Inside the toilet flushed.

Chloe's dormant headache throbbed to life again.

The door clicked open. Lindsay stepped outside, tears streaming down her cheeks. She passed the stick to Chloe. A bright blue plus sign blinked at her.

Chloe's stomach fell like an elevator on freefall. "Oh, no." She took one look at Lindsay's face and pulled her into a tight hug.

The girl's slim shoulders shook. "What am I going to do?"

"I don't know. But I'm here to help you through this. You're not alone. Come and sit down." She led the girl to the couch. "You'll have to tell your mom so she can take you to the doctor."

Lindsay twisted a tissue until it shredded.

A sick feeling of dread flowed through Chloe's stomach. "Lindsay, look at me and tell me the truth. Where is your mother?"

Lindsay bit her bottom lip. "She—she's in Kingsville for a while."

Chloe's stomach dropped again. "Working? Or living there?"

Lindsay's brown hair shielded her face. "Both."

"How long has she been gone?"

Lindsay hiccupped through her tears. "I don't know. She got a second job at a night club. At first, she'd just stay overnight with a friend. But then I found out she has a boyfriend."

"Does she come home at all?"

"She comes back every few weeks, but mostly she's gone."

"And you've been trying to keep everything going here by yourself?"

She nodded again.

Chloe's heart ached. No wonder Matt was so angry all the time. And no wonder Lindsay was always skittish and sad, keeping such an enormous secret while trying to look after herself and her brother. She'd been easy prey for any boy who would pay attention and pretend to care.

And now she was expecting a baby.

An uncommon anger burned through Chloe's system. These kids needed her help. She would not let Lindsay face this crisis alone.

Lindsay clutched Chloe's arm. "You can't tell anyone about my mom. They'll put Matt in foster care or a group home. He'd never survive that."

Aidan's words rang in Chloe's ears. *I'd have to call*

County Social Services."

What *were* her obligations? Could she keep a secret this huge from Aidan? Especially after he'd repeatedly warned her about getting too involved with the kids?

"Please, Miss Martin." Huge tears hovered on Lindsay's lower lashes.

Yet how could Chloe knowingly force Matt into foster care, almost guaranteeing that he would end up in a gang? "I'll keep quiet—for now. But I'll have to contact your mother."

Lindsay gulped. "OK."

"We'll get you through this. I promise." Chloe held the girl's shaking frame. Somehow she'd have to find a way to keep that promise.

20

Secrets, lies, and deceptions. Aidan hated them.

And Matt Brown was embroiled up to his shaggy brown hair in exactly that.

A phone call from Mike Hillier confirmed Matt was involved with a gang. One of the reasons Aidan wanted to open the youth center was to give kids alternatives. Was it too late for Matt?

Principal Jenkins knocked and entered Aidan's office. "Do you have a minute?" The large man stood inside the door.

"Of course. Sit down." Aidan's senses went on alert.

When Larry had something to say, he'd normally call Aidan to his office.

"No, thanks. I just wanted to give you fair warning that I've offered Miss Peters a temporary position for the remainder of the school year. She'll be starting next week, taking over for Mrs. Winters in the English department."

"I see." Dread filled his lungs, clogging his breath.

"I'm sympathetic to your concerns, but this will give us six months to see how things work out. By then, if you still have serious issues, we'll reevaluate for the next school year."

His throat too dry to speak, Aidan could only nod.

Larry peered over his bifocals. "I expect your full cooperation with Miss Peters. You don't have to like her to work with her."

Larry had hired him when most other schools wouldn't even grant him an interview, so Aidan didn't challenge the decision. "I understand, sir."

"Good." Larry gave a brief nod and left the office.

Aidan slumped in his chair. He thought he'd left his problems in Arizona. Now they were coming back to haunt him. *Lord, please help me deal with Patricia in a fair manner. And please don't let her create any more havoc in my life.*

The intercom buzzed, jangling his taut nerves. "Yes, Mrs. Grebbins."

"Your sister is here."

"Send her in." He came around the desk to meet Maxi as she strolled in the door. "Hey, sis." He kissed her cheek, ignoring her slight scowl. "Where's Ben?"

"Spending some quality time with his daddy."

"So how are you?"

Maxi hefted the enormous bag off her shoulder and sat down. "If you'd bother to call once in a while, you'd know."

He suppressed the urge to roll his eyes. "Sorry, I've been tied up lately."

"By a gorgeous brunette named Chloe?"

"Of course not." Immediately he regretted his sharp tone. "Sorry. I've got a lot on my mind."

"What's wrong? You don't look so hot."

"I just found out Patricia's taken a job here for the rest of the year."

Maxi's eyes widened. "You're kidding. Why would she leave a good job in Arizona for a position here? Unless she's trying to win you back."

"Yeah, well, I've made it clear I'm not interested. I just don't need the headache of having her around all the time."

"Talk about uncomfortable." Maxi crossed her arms and leaned back in the chair. "Well, if she gives you any grief, I can always unleash some sisterly fierceness on her."

Aidan chuckled. "I may take you up on that. Now what did you come by for? Not to hear my problems, I'm sure."

"I was going to give you an earful about neglecting Mama again, but now that I've heard your side, I'm prepared to cut you some slack."

Guilt sliced through him. Other than a few random phone calls, he *had* neglected his mother. During the summer, he'd seen her every week, but since school started, he'd put work ahead of everything. He scrubbed a hand over his face. "Did Mom say something to you?"

"You know she would never complain. But she did mention she hadn't seen you in a while." Maxi paused. "She's coming for lunch after church on Sunday. Why don't you come, too, and visit with all of us at once?"

"Count me in. Thanks, Max."

"You're welcome." She picked up her bag and rose. "But before I let you off the hook completely, I heard you were with Chloe at the hospital when Lily had the baby."

"That's right."

"Chloe's getting to you, isn't she?"

"Maxi—"

"Of course she is. She's gorgeous and sweet with a huge heart."

"We're just friends." Why did that statement feel like a lie? Because he'd never kissed his friends the way he'd kissed Chloe. He yanked open the door to his office.

"If you say so. But you're missing out on a great woman, and not just because she's my friend. You know..." she wiggled her brows, "... you could use her to get Patricia off your back."

Aidan seared her with his stern principal look. "I'm not getting involved with anyone, so you can stop scheming."

"OK, big brother. I get it. See you on Sunday." She patted his cheek as she swept out the door.

Aidan knew better than to trust that syrupy, sweet response. His sister was up to something. And from past experience, he probably wouldn't like it.

~*~

Chloe entered the Good Shepherd Church in a better frame of mind on Sunday. The guilt, however, still inched its way through her system. Would she ever be able to forget the past and start with a clean slate?

When Richard called, he'd told her Denise had miscarried. The baby conceived while Richard was supposedly estranged from his wife. According to him, he'd stayed with Denise for the sake of his three-year-old son and five-year-old daughter. Obviously he was far more involved than he let on. And now the child that had bound Richard more firmly to his wife was gone.

Chloe felt sorry for Denise. The woman did not deserve the grief of losing a child on top of the knowledge that her husband had been unfaithful. Chloe twisted her hands in her lap, rubbing the scar from her burn. She needed that very tangible reminder of her role in the destruction of this once intact family. No matter her innocence at the outset, she'd stayed when she ought to have left with what remained of her integrity.

She turned her attention to the lessons Nick read from the pulpit.

Passion blazed in his eyes as he spoke from the heart about God's love. "If we confess our sins, He is faithful and just and will forgive us our sins and purify us from all unrighteousness. That's from 1 John 1:9." Nick looked straight at her.

The atmosphere in the room seemed overly warm. She plucked at the neckline of her dress to allow her more air. She would not have another anxiety attack. Her last episode had occurred in church as well. Maybe the depth of her guilt was the cause—guilt that she'd managed to repress during the busyness of her week, but which rose to the surface in church. She inhaled deeply and let her breath out in slow, deliberate puffs. If she concentrated, she might be all right.

At last, the organist began the closing hymn.

Chloe rose from her seat, still breathing deeply until Nick had left the pulpit. Then she almost sagged in relief. She'd made it through the full service. When certain her legs were steady enough to walk, she made her way down the aisle to the back of the church.

Maxi broke away from the crowd to approach Chloe. "Hey. I wanted to invite you for lunch. Mama will be there and I know she'd love to see you."

Chloe smiled at the thought of Maxi's gentle mother. Despite losing her husband and suffering a debilitating disease, nothing swayed the good nature of that sweet woman. Nick was headed to the hospital to bring Lily and the baby home, and the thought of her lonely apartment did not appeal to her in the least. "Sure, I'd love to come."

"Great. See you over at the house."

~*~

Standing at Maxi's living room window, Aidan could help but notice Chloe getting out of her car. He should've known. 'Maxi the Matchmaker' was at it again.

In light of Nick's warning and Aidan's seeming inability to avoid temptation, he'd made a vow to keep an emotional distance until Chloe no longer worked at the school. Yet everyone and everything seemed destined to thwart his good intentions. Aidan decided to sit back, an impartial observer, and enjoy her company without getting personal. And make certain they were never alone. He resumed his seat beside his mother's wheelchair and took her hand.

She smiled at him, her faded blue eyes alight with love. "You look tired, dear. Are you sure you're not working too hard?"

Trust his mom to be concerned about him when she was the one battling MS. "I'm fine, Mom. How have you been? I'm sorry I haven't been around more often."

"You don't need to worry. Peg takes good care of me. And I love working at the salon."

"I'm glad. When things settle down at work, I owe you a lunch date."

"I'd like that very much." Mom smiled.

The front door opened and footsteps sounded in

the hallway.

Aidan waited for Chloe to appear. When she didn't, it took every ounce of willpower not to go looking for her.

Mom continued to regale him with stories about the customers at the hair salon.

His head jerked up the moment Chloe breezed in.

She looked stunning in her Sunday outfit, a striped blue and white dress and her usual high heels. Brunette curls cascaded past her shoulders.

His heart ground to a painful halt at the brilliant smile she gave his mother.

"Mrs. North. How wonderful to see you again." Chloe bent to kiss his mother's cheek and her perfume enveloped him.

"Chloe, my dear. You look absolutely beautiful. And please call me Bernice. Mrs. North makes me feel so old."

Chloe gave a light laugh and turned to him. "Hello, Aidan."

His tongue tangled up. This *Chloe fever* was getting worse every time he saw her.

"Lunch is ready in the dining room," Maxi called out.

Grateful for the distraction, Aidan rose to wheel his mother into the next room. He managed to grab a seat at the far end of the table away from Chloe. The meal progressed without incident. The focus of conversation stayed with Jason and the firehouse, as well as the beauty shop where Maxi, Peg, and his mother worked.

Chloe seemed to enjoy the conversation, but now and then, he caught her glancing at him and then quickly averting her gaze.

After lunch, Jason took Ben for a nap while Maxi cleared the plates.

At the sound of a muffled ringtone, Chloe pulled her phone out. Her eyes widened and the color drained from her face. She stood abruptly. "I'm sorry," she said to the room in general. "I'll have to skip dessert." She flashed a brief smile, but pinched lines formed around her mouth. Something had upset her.

"Is everything all right, dear?" Even his mother had noticed.

"Just a personal matter I have to deal with." Chloe bent to kiss her good-bye. "I'll see you again soon I hope." She lifted her gaze for a brief second to Aidan. "Tell Maxi thank you, and I'll call her later." She rushed from the room, her anxiety almost palpable.

Was Matt in trouble again? Or was Chloe the one in trouble?

Good intentions fled, and Aidan followed her out onto the porch. "Chloe. Wait up."

Either she didn't hear him or she ignored him. Before he could reach her, she jumped into her car and roared out of the driveway.

21

Richard was here in Rainbow Falls. Waiting for her in Ruby's diner.

The shock of his text message reverberated through Chloe as she drove into town. He'd texted that if she didn't meet him within the hour, he'd go to see Nick and Lily. How had he even remembered her sister's married name?

There was no way she'd let Richard talk to Nick. She had to handle this problem and get rid of him as soon as possible. Yet the thought of facing him made her hands tremble.

She parked a block away from the diner and paused to collect herself. Several deep breaths later, she got out of the car and walked toward Ruby's. The door jangled as she entered the restaurant. The familiar scent of coffee and apple pie greeted her. For mid-afternoon on a Sunday, the place was unusually quiet. Only a couple of men sat at the counter.

Richard was seated at the farthest booth in the back.

Her heart thumped when he walked toward her.

"Hello, Chloe." The deep rumble of his voice stirred long dormant memories.

Other than the lines bracketing his eyes and mouth, he looked as handsome as ever. Thin streaks of silver shone in his dark hair, a testament to the difficulties of recent months. Yet he appeared chic as always, wearing the trendiest of designer suits, accented by a striped silver and black tie.

"Hello, Richard."

He bent to kiss her cheek, and then motioned for her to sit down. Once she settled on the bench, he took a seat across from her. "You look wonderful, sweetheart. Small town life must agree with you."

She cringed at the endearment. "What are you doing here?"

He moved his cup and saucer to the side. "I needed to talk to you, but since you never answer my calls, I had to come to see you in person."

A waitress appeared at her elbow. "Can I get you something?"

"No, thank you." Heartburn and nausea clamped down on Chloe's stomach.

"I'll have a refill on my coffee, please." Richard held out his cup. He thanked her and she moved away.

"I'm sorry about the baby," Chloe said. "I imagine Denise was devastated."

"Yes. She still is."

"What about you, Richard?" She couldn't keep the bitterness out of her voice.

"To be honest, I was relieved."

She stiffened. How could he be relieved at the loss of his child?

He reached out and covered one of her cold hands. "It gave me the courage to finally leave Denise."

She pulled her hand free. "You left her—right after this kind of tragedy?"

He looked confused. "I thought that's what you wanted all along. You've been after me for months to leave her. If it hadn't been for the pregnancy…"

She drew in a sharp breath and let it hiss out.

"There never should have been a pregnancy, Richard. You swore you were staying married—in name only—for the sake of your children. You lied to me—again."

"It only happened once, I swear. A big mistake one night when I'd being drinking. She seduced me, thinking it would get me back."

At one time, Chloe would have been moved by his remorse, accepted his pitiful attempt at an explanation, and forgiven him. "I don't believe you. And even if I did, drinking is no excuse."

He hung his head, fingers twirling the cup on its saucer. "You're right. I'm sorry I gave in to such weakness. Sorry I hurt you. But you have to believe me now. My marriage is over. I've filed for divorce and Denise says she won't contest it." He paused and raised tortured eyes to hers. "I love you, Chloe, and I want to marry you."

~*~

Aidan pulled up in front of Ruby's Diner and shut off the engine. He'd followed Chloe into town and found her car parked near the restaurant.

Through the window, Aidan saw Chloe sitting across from an older, distinguished-looking man. Judging by her frown, she didn't seem to be enjoying the conversation. Did this guy have something to do with her bakery? A contractor or inspector? If so, Aidan had never seen him before. A sudden thought jolted him. *Could this be Chloe's ex?*

Aidan took the keys out of the ignition and stopped short of storming into the restaurant. He had no right to interfere in her life.

Chloe seemed engrossed in their dialogue,

gesturing with her hands. After a few minutes, she leapt to her feet.

At the look of devastation on her face, Aidan couldn't hold back. He bolted from the car and strode into the diner, keeping his gaze trained on Chloe's back.

"I can't believe you would come here now and say that."

The tears in her voice sparked an adrenaline surge through his system. His hands clenched into fists, ready to defend her if necessary.

The man, who had also risen, reached forward to snag Chloe's hand. "Think about what I said. You can reach me at the Rainbow Falls Inn." Without warning, the man pulled her toward him and locked his lips on her.

A stab of pure jealousy knifed through Aidan. He stepped forward, waiting for a sign to intervene. The thought that maybe Chloe welcomed this guy's kiss caused another jab of pain.

Chloe pounded her fist on the man's chest. He released her with a satisfied smile on his face, which Chloe promptly smacked. "Don't ever touch me again."

Relief eased the vise grip on Aidan's insides, until the guy moved toward her, anger blazing in his eyes. Swift and silent, Aidan moved up beside her. "You heard her, buddy. Back off." He didn't dare look to see Chloe's reaction. Instead he aimed a death stare at the jerk in front of him.

"Who the devil are you?"

"A friend. You're not welcome here." Chloe had an iron grip on Aidan's arm, holding him back. He ignored the pressure and reduced the distance to his opponent. Wariness crept into the other man's eyes. Aidan's fingers bit into the palm of his hands, itching to land one good punch in the guy's smug face.

"Aidan, don't." Chloe's breathless voice barely penetrated his concentration.

He never took his eyes off the enemy. "Leave. Now. And don't come back."

A sneer spread across the man's features. "So Chloe's got herself a defender. Isn't that sweet? Playing the victim again, I see. Maybe you should ask her how long she begged me to leave my wife before she finally gave up. She's not as innocent as she looks." He swung his hard gaze to Chloe. "Are you, sweetheart?"

Aidan surged forward, but Chloe held him back.

"Aidan. Don't. Please."

Why was she protecting this creep?

"I'll be in touch, Chloe." Richard calmly side-stepped Aidan, keeping just out of his reach, and walked out of the diner. Rage simmered through Aidan's system, pulsing like a living being. He dragged in a huge breath, willing the loathing and anger to dissipate.

She's not as innocent as she looks.

The words seared his brain like a brand. This is exactly what he'd feared all along. That she'd been hiding something about her relationship. Was this her secret? That she'd knowingly entered into an affair with a married man?

Huge amber eyes, flooded with tears, stared at him.

His heart cinched at the fear he saw reflected in their depths. *Just walk away*, an inner voice urged. It would be the easiest thing to do. But one way or the other, he had to know. "Is it true?" His voice sounded

152

callous even to him.

Sorrow haunted her expression. The hand on his sleeve tightened, then fell away. Her chin quivered as she bit her bottom lip. The fact that she couldn't answer his question spoke volumes. "I can explain," she said at last.

Stones of disillusion weighed like lead in his stomach. "There's nothing you can say to explain adultery. Breaking up a God-sanctioned union. Depriving children of their father..." He stepped away from the intoxicating scent of her, his lungs fighting for air. "How could you do that? To his wife? To those innocent kids? I knew you were hiding something, but I never dreamed it was something this bad."

Her anguished sob barely registered.

"You should go after him, Chloe. You two deserve each other."

22

"Here, honey. I think you could use this." The waitress set down a glass of iced tea and handed Chloe a napkin. "No man is worth that kind of grief. Believe me."

"Thank you." Embarrassed, Chloe wiped her cheeks and then crumpled the paper into a ball.

The woman looked to be in her fifties with graying brown hair and bags of weariness beneath her eyes, yet kindness shone from their faded depths. "Can I call someone for you?"

Chloe's first thought was of Aidan. But she couldn't count on him anymore. She shook her head. "I'll be fine in a few minutes."

The woman patted her arm. "Take your time, honey. Take your time."

Chloe forced back fresh tears at the irony of the situation. If Richard had proposed three months ago, she would've been the happiest woman in New York City. Now, she wanted him to leave town and never come back. The bitter aftertaste of his kiss lingered. His touch used to heat her blood. Today, it brought nothing but revulsion and shame.

Aidan had come to her defense like an avenging angel, only to fall victim to Richard's cruel accusations. Accusations she couldn't deny. The icy glass against her cheek did little to soothe her grief at the look of disgust on Aidan's face. She muffled a sob as the stark truth slammed through her.

She was in love with Aidan.

And he hated her.

Her cellphone chimed. Hoping it might be Aidan, she checked the display, but it was Maxi. Chloe slumped on the bench seat. How would she ever explain this mess to her friend? "Hi, Maxi."

"Chloe, is everything all right? Mama said you took off in a hurry—and that Aidan followed you."

"I'm sorry." Everything sharp and raw rose in her throat.

"Where are you?"

"At Ruby's."

"Stay there. I'm coming over."

Chloe owed her friend the truth—about Richard, and about her growing feelings for Aidan. She only hoped Maxi wouldn't despise her after hearing the whole story.

Ten minutes later, Maxi sat down across from her. From the alarmed look on her friend's face, Chloe must've looked a sight. Maxi gripped her hand across the table. "Whatever it is, I'm here for you."

"I got a text from Richard. He's here in Rainbow Falls."

Maxi's brows plunged down. "What did he want?"

"It's a long, ugly story. Are you sure you want to know?"

Maxi leaned on the table, her hazel eyes intense. "It's about time. Tell me everything."

Other than a few eye rolls and frowns, Maxi let Chloe talk uninterrupted until she finally ran out of words—and tears.

Maxi squeezed her hand. "I'm so sorry you had to

go through all that. What a colossal jerk the man is. Thinking he could sail into town after everything and you'd just swoon at his feet."

"I was so stupid. How did I not see what he was really like?"

"You're not the first girl to be taken in by a smooth-talking married man. And you won't be the last." She pinned her with a sharp look. "You're not still in love with him, are you?"

Chloe shook her head. "The moment I saw his wife's pregnant belly, I was done. For good."

"I get it, believe me." Maxi's anger thawed some of the ice that seemed to have encased her.

"But where does Aidan fit in? Did he follow you here?"

Chloe nodded, her lips pressed together.

"And…?"

"And…he despises me." Chloe clenched her fingers until the nails bit into her palms.

Maxi's keen eyes searched Chloe's face. "Do you have feelings for my brother?"

"It doesn't matter now."

Maxi's lips twisted up. "I'll take that as a yes. Which is a good thing since I'm pretty sure he's crazy about you too."

"Not anymore."

"Listen…I know my brother. Give him some time to cool off, and he'll come around. He'll get over this, I know it."

Maxi's firm assertion didn't spark any hope in Chloe's shriveled heart.

It would hurt too much if she was wrong.

~*~

Aidan sat in the youth center's empty gym. Sweat poured off his body, soaking his shirt. Three days after the confrontation in the diner, raw anger still burned like a hot coal. An hour of whaling a basketball at an imaginary enemy had done little to ease his rage and disillusionment. Nothing could change the stark reality of his situation.

He'd fallen in love with an adulteress. How dare she cloak herself in a veil of innocence? Lure him in with her vulnerability, her enthusiasm, and her caring heart. He never would have had anything to do with her if he'd known.

You would shun her like a leper, as though she didn't deserve to breathe the same air as you.

The words entered his mind with the force of a lance. Hadn't he been treated like a leper by the staff at the school in Arizona? By Patricia?

In disgust, Aidan stood and heaved the ball against the far wall. It ricocheted and skipped across the gym floor, coming to rest in the corner. His body reverberated with the same violent vibrations. He wanted to take a baseball bat and smash every window, destroy every light fixture, demolish everything—until the roaring agony inside him released its stranglehold. Lucky for him, the center had no bats on site. He blew out a deep breath, trying to rid his body of the rage.

He'd avoided Chloe at school, holed up in his office like a wounded bear. The true torture, however, was coming home at night, seeing her car in the driveway, and knowing she was upstairs in her apartment.

"Hello, Aidan."

He jerked around, hoping her voice was a figment of his imagination.

She stood inside the main door, hands clasped.

He allowed the pain of her presence to pulse in his veins, before he hardened his muscles like a shield. "I have nothing to say to you." He bent to pick up the ball and then strode to the equipment room in the corner.

"Well, I have something to say to you."

Each tap of her shoes across the floor slapped against his nerve endings. He hurled the ball into the cupboard, locked the door, and with no other recourse, turned to face her. "You don't want to be around me right now. Not in the mood I'm in."

"You've been avoiding me for days. Not returning my calls. I think I deserve the chance to explain myself."

"I won't listen to your lies."

Her eyes flashed. "*My* lies? You assume that Richard, a total stranger, is telling the truth, and I'm the one who's lying."

The accuracy of her statement stung like bitter acid. Suddenly he was back in the principal's office in Arizona with Emily's parents spouting falsehoods about him, and the man he looked up to, his boss and mentor, believing them without even hearing his side of the story. Wasn't he doing the same thing to Chloe? Without answering, he stalked over to his gym bag on the bench, pulled out a towel, and wiped the sweat off his face.

"I didn't know Richard was married when we started dating."

He continued to rub his arms with the towel, pretending not to listen.

"My mother had just died. Nick and Lily were

busy with their new baby, and I...I felt completely alone. In New York with no friends or family. Then Richard started pursuing me."

Aidan tossed the damp towel into his bag and pulled out a bottle of water.

"He overwhelmed me with attention, gave me gifts, and sent me love notes. I fell hard for him. For once, I was the most important person in the world to someone."

Aidan hardened his heart to the catch in her voice, to the sound of tears threatening. He twisted the cap off the bottle and drank.

"When I discovered he had a wife and kids, I—"

He whipped around, anger blazing. "You what? Begged him to leave his family?"

Her lips trembled. A large tear wound its way down, curving by her mouth and dropping from her chin. "I wanted to die." Her whisper vibrated through the empty gym. "Richard found me with a bottle of pills. He made me swear I wouldn't do anything foolish. He told me he loved me and to be patient. He wanted to leave his wife, but the timing wasn't right. He swore he would leave Denise as soon as things settled down. I believed him."

A sliver of compassion wiggled past his anger. "How long did you wait?"

"Six months. The worst six months of my life. It finally took his wife to make me see the truth."

His jaw dropped. "You went to his wife?"

"She came to me. She found out about us through someone at the restaurant. One night she waited until I was alone in the kitchen." Chloe's body shook. She sank onto the bench beside his bag, as though her legs wouldn't support her.

He waited for her to continue.

"She grabbed one of the butcher knives from the counter and came at me."

Horrible images rose in Aidan's mind. "Where was Richard?" If he'd been any kind of man, he would've stopped the affair before irreparable damage was done.

"He got there—a little too late."

"She stabbed you?"

"She tried. I grabbed her but fell back. My other hand landed against the hot stove."

What had she said about the burn? *Cooks got burned all the time.* Yeah, not by someone trying to stab them. "You didn't deserve that."

A mixture of sorrow and guilt swirled in her eyes. "Didn't I? I thought I did."

"What happened then?"

"She came at me again, but Richard arrived and got the knife away from her. It was then that I noticed Denise was several months pregnant."

Aidan struggled to comprehend. "You mean…"

She gave a bitter laugh. "That's right. The whole time he was supposed to be leaving her, he'd gotten her pregnant instead." She stood and wrapped her arms around her torso. "Something died in me that night."

"Did you press charges?"

"No. I couldn't deprive the children of their mother. I told Richard to take her home and never speak to me again. The next day, my boss fired me."

The anger whooshed out of him like a balloon losing air. "What a mess."

Chloe pulled out a tissue. She wiped her nose and lifted her chin, a bit of spirit returning to her demeanor. "Just so you know, I sent Richard home."

Despite everything, a flare of jealousy shot through him. "You went to his hotel room?"

Annoyance flashed. "Of course not. I spoke to him on the phone."

"How do you know he's gone?"

"Nick made sure he left."

"Nick knew about this?"

"Not all of it." A wry smile twisted her lips. "Even though he's a minister, he does have a temper. I was afraid he'd put Richard in the hospital."

Aidan's jaw tightened. "I know the feeling."

She pulled the strap of her purse over her shoulder. "I wanted you to understand the reasons behind what I did. I'm not proud of that chapter of my life, but I'm doing everything I can to start over."

A fresh start. Isn't that why he came back to Rainbow Falls? To escape the dark shadows of his past? He zipped up his gym bag and straightened. "The only way you'll be able to do that, Chloe, is to ask for God's forgiveness and make amends for any harm you've caused."

She went very still. "And what about your forgiveness, Aidan? How do I earn that?"

He shook his head sadly, defeat creeping through his system. "I'm sorry. I don't know if that's even possible."

23

After school the next day, Chloe and Lindsay washed out cupboards in the kitchen at the bakery.

Chloe kept a careful eye on Lindsay. The girl was in the first trimester of her pregnancy, and Chloe's mission was to keep her healthy, both emotionally and physically. Focusing on Lindsay and the bakery had the added benefit of keeping Chloe's depression at bay. As well as her irritation over the deplorable lack of concern Mrs. Brown had shown when Chloe had talked to her.

She had finally managed to reach the woman earlier that day, only to be told in no uncertain terms—peppered with very colorful language—to mind her own business. And leave her kids alone.

Unfortunately, Chloe's conscience would not allow her to do that. She'd keep trying to get Mrs. Brown to see reason, even if she had to track her down in Kingsville to do it.

Loud music poured from the radio in the restaurant area. Matt had repainted the walls to cover up the offensive red slashes. Now that his work at the youth center was finished, he'd started working at Chloe's shop. The extra help was proving a Godsend to her. She should be ready to open by December.

Lindsay threw her rag into the bucket. "I'm finished with these cupboards. Do you want me to unpack the boxes?"

"Sure. If the bottom drawers are dry, you can put the baking tins away." Chloe resumed scrubbing. Physical activity helped keep her from thinking about Aidan. She hoped one day he could forgive her, but in the meantime, praying seemed the only avenue left. She needed to have patience and trust in God's timing.

Lindsay straightened from opening a carton, one hand on her stomach, the other over her mouth.

Concern shot through Chloe. "Nauseous?"

"A little."

Chloe crossed to the fridge and pulled out a bottle of water. "Here, this will help."

Lindsay took the bottle, sank onto a stool by the counter, and drank.

Chloe waited until a bit of color returned to her cheeks.

"Have you talked to Dylan again?" He hadn't taken the news well, but Chloe had urged Lindsay to try again, once he'd had some time to digest the idea of a pregnancy.

"Not really."

Chloe held back a sigh. Lindsay needed unconditional support, not pressure. "You've got lots of time. He may come around."

Lindsay raised solemn eyes to Chloe. "The truth is, Miss Martin, I broke up with Dylan before I found out I was pregnant. He's pretty immature, and he was always looking at other girls."

Chloe's tongue refused to work. She stared at the girl.

"I let him know about the baby. But I don't expect anything else from him."

Chloe was amazed at Lindsay's maturity. The fact that she'd recognized Dylan to be unsuitable spoke volumes. "Sounds like you've given this a lot of thought."

"I have." Lindsay gave a soft smile. "I want to keep the baby and raise it on my own."

"That's incredibly brave of you." Chloe slid a box across the floor, thinking how different the girl's future would be.

When she turned, Lindsay was staring at her. "I have a favor to ask, Miss Martin."

"Sure. What is it?"

A flush colored the girl's pale cheeks. "Our rent is overdue and my mom isn't answering my calls. Would you be able to...lend us the money until she comes with her paycheck?"

Lindsay shouldn't have to deal with all these grown up problems at her age.

"I tell you what. Let me talk to your mother. If I can't get her to come back and pay the rent, I'll make sure it's covered."

Lindsay hesitated, and then gave a jerky nod. "OK. But you'll have to do it soon. I don't know how much longer the landlord will wait."

The bell jangled out front.

Chloe whirled around. Hadn't Matt locked the door?

Ever since the break-in, Chloe had been extra diligent with keeping the doors bolted. Her hands shook as she lowered the cloth into the bucket of soapy water. The sound of a baritone voice talking to Matt registered in Chloe's consciousness, turning her terror to annoyance. *Not again.* With deliberate calm, she dried her hands on a towel, stiffened her spine, and marched out to the front room.

Richard's gaze snapped to her. "Chloe, there you

are."

The sight of him looking smug in another designer suit only fueled Chloe's irritation. "I thought you'd gone back to New York."

"I want to talk to you. In private, if possible." He shot a glance at Matt who had resumed painting.

She might as well get this conversation over with and sever the ties for good. "Matt, can you break down the boxes in the alley for me?"

Matt stopped rolling the paint. "Now?"

"Yes, please."

He dropped the roller into the tray and wiped his hands on a rag hanging from his jeans. "You OK with this guy?"

"I'll be fine. Give us five minutes."

Matt threw Richard a warning glare, and then stalked toward the alley door.

"Make it quick, Richard. I have work to do."

He strolled around the room, eyeing the newly restored wicker furniture and the glass display cases. "You've come a long way *down* from *Oliver's*."

Irritation prickled along her spine. "I'm sure you didn't come here to comment on my shop. What do you want?"

He turned his attention to her. "I'm not giving up on us, Chloe. I'm willing to do whatever it takes."

Part of her wished she could still be that naïve woman, waiting for Richard to sweep her away. If her priorities hadn't changed so much since coming back here, she could've returned to New York and become Mrs. Richard Highmore as she'd dreamed.

Richard reached inside his suit jacket and brought out a black velvet box.

Her breath hitched as he flipped the lid to reveal

the blaze of a multi-carat diamond.

"Marry me, Chloe. We'll start a whole new life together. Just you and me. If it's a bakery you want, I'll find you one in Manhattan. We'll be a team, working together."

He was saying everything she'd ever wanted him to say and more. Only it had come much too late. No longer would she settle for a man who thought nothing of cheating, of losing a child, and of leaving his wife to handle everything alone.

Shame burned that she had once been selfish enough to ask him to do just that. Now Chloe wanted more. She wanted a life pleasing to God, helping kids like Lindsay and Matt reach their full potential. And someday, God willing, she wanted the love of a good man, an honorable man.

A man like Aidan North.

She took the box. With a wistful sigh for what might have been, she ran a finger over the diamond, and then snapped the lid shut. "I'm sorry, Richard. I can't marry you." She pressed the box into his hand, surprised at the tremor in his fingers. At first, she thought it was grief, but when she raised her gaze, anger blazed in his eyes.

"You have the nerve to refuse me? After everything I've sacrificed for you?"

She fought the urge to cower and stuck out her chin. "Go back to your wife, Richard. Work things out with Denise. For the kids' sake."

"I don't want Denise. I want you. That fact was never in question—until you gave up too soon."

Her nerves twisted into a whipcord of anger. "Waiting for you almost cost me my life. In more ways than one." Her breathing came in shallow puffs. "I think you'd better leave before we both say something we'll regret."

"It's that guy from the diner, isn't it? You've got a thing for him."

She stiffened, pressing her lips together.

He scoffed. "I'm guessing Mr. Outraged won't give you the time of day now that he knows what kind of a woman you really are." He went on, spouting foul names at her.

"Stop it," she said evenly. "There are children here who do not need to hear that. But then again, you don't care much about children, do you? Not even your own."

He landed a blow before she could blink. The force of the impact threw her across the floor. Tears smarted as blood squirted from her nose. She held a hand to her throbbing cheek, moisture almost blinding her.

"You better leave, mister." Matt appeared with one of her largest butcher knives gripped in his hand.

Dear God, no. She scrambled to her feet. "It's OK, Matt. He's leaving now."

Richard froze, eyes glued to the blade. Then the air hissed out between his teeth, and the anger seemed to drain from his face. "If that's the way you want it, Chloe. We could have had a great life." Richard stomped out the door, the bell jangling.

Chloe's knees shook. She leaned on the counter as the adrenaline seeped out, leaving her as limp as an overcooked noodle.

"Come on." Matt led her toward the kitchen. "Get some ice, Linds. Her lip is swelling."

Lindsay stood in the doorway. "Who was that man?"

Chloe winced at the horrified expression on the

girl's face. "My ex-boyfriend."

Matt dragged a chair over, and Lindsay brought a wet cloth filled with ice cubes.

Chloe placed the cool pack on her cheek and lip.

"We should call the police." Lindsay's voice quivered.

"No." The word erupted almost of its own volition. "Richard's gone for good this time. Let's leave it at that." A puffy lip and a bloody nose were well worth the price to be rid of him.

She never wanted to hear the name Richard Highmore again.

24

"Good morning, Mr. North. I have your messages for you."

Aidan scowled at Mrs. Grebbins's cheery tone. What was she doing here at just past seven? He'd come in early to get some peace and quiet before the craziness of the day began. He stopped at her desk. "Anything urgent?"

"Not really. The fundraising chair called to remind you about the upcoming bake sale. They'd like the home economics class to provide most of the baking. And speaking of the home ec class, Miss Martin called in sick this morning."

Aidan stopped flipping through the messages. He looked at Mrs. Grebbins and forced his expression to remain neutral. "Did she say what was wrong?"

"Just that she was under the weather."

"Guess the baking will have to wait until she returns."

"Oh, and you have someone waiting in your office."

Visions of Patricia leapt to mind. He'd managed to avoid her, but he knew sooner or later she'd corner him. In his already sour mood, he didn't have the patience for her manipulations.

"It's Lindsay Brown. She seemed upset, so I let her wait inside."

The tension drained from his shoulders. A student

he could deal with. "That's fine. Thank you, Mrs. Grebbins."

Inside his office, Lindsay sat slumped in his guest chair.

"Good morning, Lindsay. What can I do for you?" Aidan stepped behind his desk and laid his briefcase on the clean surface, hoping Matt hadn't gotten into any more trouble.

"Mr. North, I need to tell you something. It's about Miss Martin."

Aidan's head snapped up, and he noted Lindsay's pale face, her freckles standing out on her cheeks. He took his seat, muscles tense. "Is something wrong? I know she called in sick today."

"She's not really sick. I promised I wouldn't say anything, but I'm scared." Moisture created a sheen in Lindsay's eyes.

The headache that had brewed at his temples all morning now banged to life. He rubbed a hand across his forehead. "Why are you scared?"

She plucked a loose thread on her jeans. "Miss Martin's old boyfriend came to see her at the bakery yesterday." She paused, rocking slightly in her chair. "They argued and he…he hit her. Knocked her across the floor. It was awful." A tear spilled over and trailed down to her chin.

The words struck like an arrow to Aidan's heart. It took all his willpower to remain in his seat. He pushed a box of tissues across the desk. "I thought the man had left town."

Lindsay dabbed her eyes. "Well, he was there yesterday. Matt grabbed a knife from the kitchen and made him leave. I watched from the back, but I didn't do anything to help her." She sobbed into the tissue, her shoulders heaving.

"It's normal to be scared, Lindsay. Especially faced with such violent anger."

She hiccupped and blew her nose.

"Did anyone call the police?"

"No, Miss Martin wouldn't let us." The tissue became a wadded ball in her hand. "I thought maybe you could check on her and make sure she's OK—in case he comes back again."

Raw emotion filled him, but he refused to allow it to surface. He wouldn't upset the girl any further. "Thank you for telling me, Lindsay. I'll take care of it."

~*~

Chloe stirred a bowl of batter in her galley kitchen, venting her frustrations with the whip of her arm. She'd had to call in sick to work. She couldn't face the kids—or Aidan—with bruises makeup couldn't conceal. She hoped she'd be able to go back to work tomorrow. The cold packs had already reduced the swelling in her lip and nose.

Alone and restless, Chloe had turned to baking— the one activity which always brought her solace. She'd make some recipes to use for the fundraiser the kids told her would be happening next week.

The stomp of heavy footsteps on the landing made her heart rate gallop. Had Richard come back? But no, he couldn't have gotten in the front door. A shaky breath escaped her. It had to be Aidan—or Nick. The only other people with a key.

Loud knocks hammered her door. "Chloe, open up. I know you're not sick."

Aidan. Maybe if she ignored him, he'd think she

was asleep and leave her in peace.

The banging resumed.

"I—I'm not feeling well, Aidan," she called. "Can't it wait until tomorrow?"

"No. And you can cut the act. Lindsay told me the whole story."

The wooden spoon slipped from her hand and landed with a plop on the floor. "Just a minute." Her hands shook as she wiped the floor. Her mind whirled, searching for a way out. She dried her hands on her apron, and then released her hair clip, arranging it to hide her cheek. She crossed to the door, unlocked the bolt, and opened it with the chain still on. "What are you doing here?"

"I came to see what kind of damage that jerk did."

"There's nothing to see."

She pushed the door closed, but he jammed his foot in the opening.

"Let me in. Or would you rather I get Nick to come over?"

"No." Bracing for the inevitable, she unhooked the chain, and opened the door. She stood back, saying nothing as Aidan entered.

His dark brows drew together in a scowl. "Let me see." He brushed the hair away from her cheek.

The warmth of his hand on her face and the familiar scent of his aftershave made her long to bury her face into his shoulder.

"That scum did this to you?"

She stepped out of his grip. "Yes."

His eyes blazed. "I thought he was gone, or did you lie about that too?"

She absorbed the pain of his sarcasm without flinching. "As far as I know, he did leave. But he came back. With a ring." She escaped into the sanctuary of her kitchen.

"He proposed? Then assaulted you?" Aidan hovered in the kitchen doorway, his fists clenched.

"He wasn't too happy when I refused his offer." She rinsed off the wooden spoon and resumed her stirring.

He crossed his arms over his chest. "Why did you turn him down? Isn't that what you wanted all along?"

His harsh tone tore at her vulnerable heart. "Not anymore. I don't want the same things I used to."

Aidan filled the small space with this formidable presence. "What *do* you want, Chloe?"

His husky voice brought goose bumps out on her arms.

I want you. She couldn't very well blurt that out. Instead she offered him her new truth. "I want to live a life in keeping with God's will. I want a partner who treats me with respect. And I want to make a positive contribution to the community. Live a life that would make my parents proud." When she risked a glance at Aidan, his expression gave nothing away. She bent to pull baking tins from the cupboard under the sink.

"Why didn't you charge him with assault?" His tone was accusing, almost callous.

"Because I wanted him to go away. Lindsay and Matt were there, and I was concerned for their safety."

The stiffness of his shoulders relaxed. "You're right, the kids didn't need to be mixed up in that."

All the shame and guilt rose up. She'd let the depravity of her past taint her life here in her hometown. "I'll spend the rest of my life trying to make up for the suffering I've caused." Tears blurred her vision as she fought hard to regain her composure.

Aidan came up behind her. Warm hands turned her around, pulling her into his chest. "You made a mistake—granted a big one—but you shouldn't have to pay for it your whole life."

Chloe buried her face in the fabric of his jacket, and wept. Encircled in the warmth of his arms, his heart beating a steady rhythm beneath her cheek, she wished she could stay in this haven forever. When the storm of tears subsided, she pulled away from his shoulder.

He handed her a tissue to wipe her face.

"Do you think you might be able to forgive me...one day?" She stared at the floor, not brave enough to see the answer on his face.

A finger touched her chin, forcing her to look up.

Heated emotions swirled in his eyes. "I forgive you, Chloe. I'm just not sure I can ever trust you."

25

Back in his office, Aidan slumped into his chair. Once again, he'd allowed his emotions to override his common sense. What had he been thinking charging over to Chloe's apartment?

He'd wanted—no *needed*—to see that she was all right. The sight of her battered face had blown away his defenses, bringing the feelings he thought he'd finally managed to subdue back to the surface.

He groaned and ran his hands through his hair. Why did his good judgment vanish every time he was with her? Being in love made him weak, made him ignore his logic. Chloe turned those big brown eyes on him, and he'd melted.

Aidan stared out his office window. For now, he would give her the benefit of the doubt. But somehow he needed to guard his heart. She would have to prove her sincerity before he'd let his walls down again.

A knock forced his thoughts back to the present. "Come in."

Patricia strolled in. "Hello, Aidan. Are you busy?"

His stomach clenched at the sight of her perfect hair and make-up, reinforcing his perception that he had terrible judgment in women. Of course, he'd dated Patricia at a time when his faith meant little, tucked away to be taken out when convenient. Now, he wouldn't even consider a relationship with a woman unless she shared his spirituality. "I have a few minutes to spare. How are you settling in?"

"Very well. I love the small town feel here."

"That's good since it looks like you'll be here for a while." He tried not to grimace. "So, what can I do for you?"

"I came by to invite you to dinner on Friday. I'd love to show you my new apartment."

Surely Larry had explained his views on employee relationships, especially since he knew their history. "I'm sorry, Patricia, but our affiliation has to remain strictly professional."

She pouted. "Can't two old friends share a meal and catch up?"

"That's not a good idea."

An uncomfortable silence filled the room.

Her blue eyes glittered with a sudden hardness. "Word has it you've been spending a lot of time with Miss Martin. Is that the reason you have no use for me?"

The coffee in his stomach soured. Patricia had only been here a few days and already she'd stirred up rumors. "Miss Martin and I have been working together to open a youth center. She and the kids are helping me renovate the building."

Patricia leaned back and crossed her legs. "So, you're not dating her?"

"No." He stacked some papers into a pile. "Is there anything else? I have a phone call to make."

Despite his dismissive tone, her expression softened. "Are you seeing anyone else right now?"

"No."

She smiled, not bothering to hide the predatory gleam. "Then nothing's stopping us from spending quality time together on school projects. Starting with this bake sale coming up. I'm adding my name to the volunteer list right now." Her skirt swished as she rose and sashayed toward the door. "See you around, Mr. North."

~*~

Chloe pulled into the parking lot of the Lucky Times Tavern, her stomach sinking at the sight of the run-down brick building sprayed with graffiti. The dread that had been crawling up her spine on the drive in to Kingsville now intensified.

At this time of day, Mrs. Brown's place of employment should be relatively empty. Chloe didn't want an audience for this conversation.

She took a quick look in the rearview mirror. Her bruises, though faded, still gave her face a sickly, yellow glow. She sighed and hoped that the lighting inside would be dim enough to hide it.

With her heart pumping as loud as the music pouring out of the rickety wooden door, Chloe stepped inside and squinted in the smoke-filled interior. Several burly men sat at the bar, while only a couple of people dotted the tables.

The man behind the bar pinned Chloe with a suspicious stare. "Can I help you, miss?"

Chloe crossed the room. "I'd like to speak with Dorothy Brown. Is she here?"

"You a police officer?" The man wiped his hand on his already stained apron.

"No. I'm here on behalf of her kids."

He turned to yell over his shoulder. "Hey, Dot. Someone out here to see you."

Chloe squirmed. The eyes of every patron focused

on her. She tightened her grip on the strap of her purse.

A few seconds went by. The doors from the kitchen to the bar swung open. A tall, thin woman scanned the area until she spotted Chloe.

"Mrs. Brown?"

The woman's eyes narrowed. "Who wants to know?"

Chloe smiled, hoping to put her at ease. "I'm Chloe Martin. We spoke on the phone the other day."

Mrs. Brown came out from behind the bar, her low-cut T-shirt clinging to her slight frame, her straight brown hair pulled back in a hair net. "I thought I made myself clear. My kids are none of your business."

The men at the bar leaned toward them, clearly interested in what might become a cat fight.

"Unfortunately that's not true, Mrs. Brown. If the children have been abandoned, I have a duty to inform social services." Chloe willed her gaze to stay even, hoping for some leverage in this conversation.

"I haven't abandoned anyone. I'm working hard to keep a roof over those kids' heads." Mrs. Brown crossed her arms in a combative stance.

"Is there somewhere more private we could talk?"

Mrs. Brown jerked her head toward the back. She turned to the bartender. "I'm taking five, Al," she called, and then marched across the room.

Chloe followed her to a corner booth and slid across the ripped vinyl seat, the odor of stale beer assaulting her.

Mrs. Brown pulled a package of cigarettes and a lighter out of her apron pocket. "Do you mind?"

"No." If it would keep the woman here for a few minutes, it was worth the second-hand smoke. Chloe folded her hands on top of the sticky table. "I thought you should know that Matt and Lindsay are in some trouble."

"What kind of trouble?" Mrs. Brown blew out a stream of smoke.

Chloe quickly filled her in.

"My baby's pregnant?" The woman's eyes rounded in horror.

"I'm afraid so." Chloe leaned forward. "She needs her mother."

"What am I supposed to do? Both my jobs are here in Kingsville. I tried to get the kids to come with me, but they refused to move. I've been staying with a…friend, and trying to go home when I can. It's not often I have the same days off from each job." Mrs. Brown's face crumpled.

"I see you're trying your best. But the apartment is filthy, and the rent is overdue. Lindsay really doesn't need all this added stress."

"I don't know what to do." Mrs. Brown's voice wobbled and moisture rimmed her eyes. "If I take time off, I won't get paid, and I could lose both jobs." Her hands shook as she took a long draw on her cigarette.

"Are there any other relatives who could help out?"

"My parents are in Oregon. But they're both in their eighties and not in good health."

"What about the kids' father?"

Mrs. Brown's lips formed a grim line. "I have no idea where he is. Haven't heard from him since he took off ten years ago. And before you ask, his parents are both dead."

Lindsay hadn't exaggerated when she said they had no family.

Chloe took a deep breath for courage. "Mrs. Brown, what if Matt and Lindsay stay with me for a while?"

Her eyes narrowed. "Why would you do that? You barely know my kids."

"I see a lot of myself in Lindsay, and I don't want Matt to get in any more trouble or possibly end up in jail."

Mrs. Brown's chin quivered. "I don't want that either."

"If you could come into town long enough to pay the rent and take Lindsay to the doctor, I'll take care of the rest. I'll pay to get the apartment into livable condition and the kids can stay with me until then."

Mrs. Brown snuffed out her cigarette in an ashtray on the table. "I guess I can get a few hours off on Sunday. I'll come then." She looked Chloe in the eye for the first time without animosity. "Thank you, Miss Martin. I'll do whatever I can to make things right for my kids."

~*~

Aidan pushed through the door of the Cut 'N Curl salon after school on Wednesday, taking note of the happy orange walls and the starburst clock on the wall. A loud Frank Sinatra tune blared from the speakers in each corner of the shop.

His mother looked up from the reception desk with a wide smile. "Aidan. What a nice surprise."

"Hi, Mom." He bent to kiss her cheek and dropped a paper bag on the desk top. "I brought you a treat from Ruby's."

"Jelly-filled donuts?"

"Of course." He grinned.

"You'll spoil my dinner, but it will be worth it."

Aidan slid a chair over and straddled it. "I came to tell you that my youth center is going to open soon."

"That's wonderful, dear. Do you think a lot of boys and girls will use it?"

"I hope so. We're planning a big opening night to get the kids out. It's next Friday. You and Peg are welcome to drop by if you'd like."

"Sounds like fun. Will Chloe Martin be there?"

A blast of heat hit Aidan's neck. Where had that come from? "Sure," he answered, careful to keep his tone even. "She's a big part of why this center is opening so soon."

"She's a lovely young woman, don't you think?" The twinkle of mischief in her eyes made Aidan squirm.

"Yes, Mom. She's a good friend."

"A friend. Well, that's a start." She pulled a donut from the bag.

"Has Maxi been filling your head with nonsense?" He scanned the shop but didn't see his sister.

"Maxine has been keeping me up to date. I believe your ex-girlfriend is working at your school."

"Unfortunately, yes."

"Please don't tell me you're getting back with her."

"No, Mom. I won't repeat that mistake."

Her whole demeanor brightened. "Thank heavens. Maybe Maxine is right, and you and Chloe will end up together."

"I think I may have to kill my sister."

"Promise me something, Aidan." She took his hand in hers.

"What is it?"

"Promise you won't harden your heart to the possibility of love. I'm certain God has someone special in mind for you, if you'll only stay open to His will."

Why was letting go and allowing God to take over so difficult? "I'll try, Mom."

She gave a serene smile. "That's a start and that's all God needs. I'll pray for the rest to follow."

~*~

"Our cupcakes are a hit, Miss Martin." Lindsay's flushed face beamed.

"Thanks to your secret ingredient, I think. The chocolate chip ones are in big demand."

The cafeteria filled with a steady stream of hungry teens eager for sweets. Standing behind the table, Chloe enjoyed the satisfaction of a job well done.

"I've learned chocolate makes almost anything irresistible." Lindsay laughed.

"You're right." Chloe grinned as she deposited some bills into the cash box.

Aidan came through the cafeteria doors. His gaze flew to hers before he turned away.

Chloe's stomach twisted. Would she ever regain his trust and respect?

"Hey, Miss Martin," Tommy called. "You have change for a twenty?"

"Sure, Tommy. Bring it over." She pulled some smaller bills from the box.

When she looked up, the blonde woman who'd kissed Aidan stood in front of her.

"You must be the infamous Miss Martin."

Somehow it didn't sound like a compliment.

"That's right."

"I'm Patricia Peters. The new English teacher. Nice to meet you." Even though the woman wore a polite smile, her blue eyes remained cold.

"Likewise."

"I'm here to help. Put me to work."

Patricia's name wasn't on her copy of the roster. "Thanks for the offer, but we've got it covered."

Patricia's face grew hard. "I told Mr. North I'd be volunteering. Didn't he tell you?"

Chloe blinked. "No, he didn't. But there's no need—"

The woman made her way behind the table, pulling an apron from one of the chairs. "More hands are always welcome." She started talking with the students.

Chloe sighed, resolving to stay as far away from Patricia Peters as possible.

"Aidan, over here." Patricia's voice rang out.

A flush covered Aidan's cheeks as he made his way to the table.

"I saved a plate of brownies for you." Patricia waved a small container. "I know they're your favorite."

"Um—thanks." He pulled his wallet out of his back pocket. "How much do I owe you?"

She gave an overloud laugh. "I think the vice-principal would want to donate at least ten dollars. Don't you, Miss Martin?"

Aidan didn't look up. His stiff posture and reddened cheeks gave evidence of his discomfort.

"I'm sure Mr. North will pay the fair price. Which isn't ten dollars." Chloe hadn't meant to challenge the woman. It just slipped out.

"Ten dollars is fine." Aidan pushed a bill at Patricia and grabbed the brownies. "Excuse me. I have to get back to work." He strode across the cafeteria and out the door.

Patricia moved so close their arms brushed. "Maybe you're not aware, but Mr. North and I used to work together in Arizona."

"I know. He told me."

"Then you know that we were almost engaged." Eyebrows rose over hard blue eyes. "I'm giving you fair warning, Miss Martin. I intend to get him back."

"Aidan and I are friends and colleagues, nothing more." Chloe held her temper in check. What Aidan did was none of her business.

"Good. Then we've got nothing to worry about." Patricia's smug smile gave Chloe the distinct impression she might have a lot to worry about.

26

Nerves fluttered in Chloe's stomach as she dressed for the youth center opening on Friday. For the teens, it would be a fun night to socialize and find out what the facility would offer. With free food, games, and a contest to name the center, Chloe hoped a lot of kids would show up—out of curiosity if nothing else.

Chloe also hoped the evening would mark a turning point with Aidan, and perhaps bring a return to their former closeness. She'd done her best to help make his dream come true, soliciting every parent and business for donations of equipment or money to furnish the center. She prayed that her new, positive changes were where God intended her to be. And perhaps, if God willed, one of the changes would be that she and Aidan might become more than friends.

Over the course of the coming weekend, she planned to move Lindsay and Matt in with her. She'd need a bed in the spare room for Matt. Lindsay could have her room, and Chloe would take the pull out couch in the living room. She'd already lined up a cleaning crew and a pest control expert to make the Browns' apartment habitable. She still had to speak to the kids and make sure they were OK with the idea. And once she received permission from Lindsay to tell Aidan about the pregnancy, Chloe would be done keeping secrets. Her spirits soared at the thought.

In her bedroom, she shifted to see her full image in

the mirror. She'd chosen the royal blue dress, wanting to make a memorable impression this evening with parents and sponsors, and to be honest, with Aidan too. A swirling mass of silk, the dress hugged her figure like a second skin and flared out at her knees. Her hair was swept up on top of her head, held in place with a rhinestone clip. She felt like a modern Cinderella, complete with high-heeled silver sandals. Though the kids would likely be dressed in jeans and T-shirts, she couldn't pass up the opportunity to glam up.

A knock echoed and Chloe's heart thudded.

Aidan had insisted on driving tonight.

Chloe was grateful that the ease of their friendship seemed to have returned. She grabbed her clutch purse and ran to open the door.

Aidan stood on the dimly lit landing. His mouth dropped open. "Wow. You look beautiful."

"Thanks. You look nice yourself."

In a navy suit and tie, with his dark hair swept back from his forehead, the outfit accentuated his gray eyes. "Are you ready?"

"Just need to grab my coat."

Aidan stepped forward to help her. His fingers lingered on her shoulder for a brief moment. When she turned, their gazes locked, and for a second, her pulse jumped at the hope he might kiss her.

With a look of regret, he stepped back. "We'd better get going."

"Sure." She belted the sash on her coat and picked up her purse and keys. Seated in the car on their way to the center, Chloe sensed a barely concealed tension in Aidan. "Are you nervous about tonight?"

"A little."

"I'm sure you'll have a good turn out."

"I hope so." His half-smile revealed a hint of vulnerability.

They'd planned to be the first ones there to double check everything and greet the teens as they arrived.

When Aidan snapped on the lights, Chloe gasped in delight. The kids had done a fabulous job decorating for the festivities. Balloons and streamers swirled from the ceiling. A disco ball in the middle of the gym shot out a kaleidoscope of colors around the room, giving it an other-worldly atmosphere.

"It looks amazing," Chloe breathed.

"Yes, it does." He turned to her. "I want to thank you, Chloe, for everything you've done. You're the reason the center is becoming a reality."

The warmth of his praise as well as the intensity of his gaze made Chloe's pulse stutter. "You're welcome. I'm only glad I could do something for you—"

The main door flew open, and a group of noisy kids piled into the hall.

He gave an apologetic shrug and went to greet them.

Chloe tried to level the giddy, breathless feeling Aidan evoked. With the kids arriving, she'd have to keep her feelings from showing. Patricia would probably make an appearance tonight, and Chloe wanted no hint of gossip.

"Wow, Miss Martin. You look awesome." Daphne's bright pink lips formed an 'o'.

"Thank you, Daphne. You look lovely too." The girls had chosen to wear nicer clothing, though most of the boys wore jeans.

Daphne laughed and pulled Lindsay into the room.

"Hi, Lindsay," Chloe said, "How are you doing tonight?"

"Fine, Miss Martin." Dressed in a slim green dress, her hair held back with a pearl clip, Lindsay exuded a simple charm.

"Is Matt coming?"

"I think so. I dropped him at a friend's house so they could come together." Her gaze darted around the room, as though searching for someone. Dylan perhaps? Was Lindsay really as over him as she claimed?

~*~

Aidan leaned against the far wall, taking a second to savor the moment. The evening had progressed just as he'd hoped.

Thirty or forty kids had turned up, and everyone seemed enthusiastic. Snatches of conversations indicated the boys planned to come back and play basketball. Others admired the games room, fitted with a Ping-Pong table, video games, a music system, and a high definition TV—all obtained thanks to the numerous calls Chloe had made to parents and other members of the community. Comfy couches, books, magazines, and two donated laptops rounded out the space.

Aidan's dream had become a reality—thanks to Chloe's contagious enthusiasm, which had convinced many parents and teachers to join the team.

His gaze strayed to Chloe, as it had most of the night. She was vibrant in her shimmering dress, talking to some of the girls at the side of the dance floor. He'd danced with her a couple of times but worried about overdoing it in case it caused too much attention.

The main door swung open, and Patricia entered. She immediately shed her red coat, revealing a matching short dress beneath.

Aidan gave a silent groan and fought the urge to hide.

She scanned the crowd, and when her gaze lit on him, she headed straight across the room. "Congratulations, Aidan. You've done a wonderful job here." She kissed his cheek.

He stepped away. "Thank you. I didn't expect you here tonight."

"I wanted to see what the hype was about. This place is important to you, so it's important to me."

It took all his willpower not to roll his eyes.

"Can I get a tour?" She batted what looked like false lashes.

"There's not much more, except the games room."

"Oh, I'd love to see it." She practically dragged him toward the end of the gym.

Conscious of Chloe's gaze, he untangled his arm from Patricia's grasp and led the way.

Several young couples jumped apart when they entered the room. His scowl sent them scurrying. *Where was the chaperone that was supposed to be in here?* Aware that he and Patricia were now alone, he wished for something to bring the others back.

Patricia examined the room. "Very nice. These kids don't know how lucky they are."

"A lot of this is due to Miss Martin's hard work. She got people to donate most of the equipment in here."

Patricia's expression soured. "Seems Miss Martin is multi-talented."

"Yes, she is. The teens will miss her when she leaves."

"Too bad for them—but not for you."

He frowned. "What does that mean?"

She trailed her hand over the back of the sofa. "Admit it, Aidan. You want to date her."

He kept his gaze steady though his insides churned. "My relationship with Miss Martin is my business."

"She has you blind-sided, Aidan. If you're not careful, she'll break your heart."

"Like you did?"

She stiffened. "How could I break your heart when you never loved me? If you had, you would've given me another chance."

He shook his head, his jaw tight. "You baled on me the second things got difficult. What kind of love is that?"

A gleam leapt in her eyes. "You're right. I made a mistake, and I want to make up for it."

Before he could react, she grabbed him for a hard kiss. Every muscle in his body froze. He pushed her away, swiping his mouth with the back of his hand. "Try that again and I'll report you for sexual harassment." He stalked past her, but turned at the doorway. "In the future, I want no contact with you unless you have a work-related issue." He ignored the tears that bloomed. "And stay out of my personal life."

Fury sat in his chest like a pent-up beast. Aidan took a long breath and forced his anger down. He would not allow Patricia to ruin this night. Heedless of the blaring music and the kids dancing, he made his way across the room to where Chloe stood. His irritation melted away in the radiance of her admiring gaze.

Her smile turned to a frown. "Is everything OK?"

"A minor run in with Patricia. Nothing to worry about." His hand itched to intertwine with hers, but instead he stuffed them in his pockets.

"I hate to say it, but that woman rubs me the wrong way."

"You're not the only one. Sometimes I wonder what I ever saw in her."

"I know what you mean." Her features brightened, and she smiled. "So, is it time to announce the contest winner yet?"

He laughed, the muscles in his stomach uncoiling. "Let me guess. You entered the draw."

"Of course I did. I had several brilliant ideas."

He laughed again and let the last vestiges of tension drain away.

~*~

A wave of pure happiness washed over Chloe. Never had she felt so in sync with someone. Not just Aidan, but the whole community. She loved helping to open this youth center—giving kids a sense of belonging and hope for a different kind of life. Judging from the turnout, this place would be a great success. She cheered when Matt's entry won the contest. If anyone deserved to name the center, he did. He embodied the type of youth this project would help. And the name he'd picked, *Aspirations*, had just the right ring of promise for the future.

Matt's friend, Jim, a boy who looked wholesome enough, clapped Matt on the back when he won. And a shy girl who'd been hanging around Matt most of the night beamed with pleasure.

Thank you, Lord. I think Matt is moving away from the gang and making friends with kids his own age.

Someone came up beside her.

"If you don't stay away from Aidan, I'll be in the principal's office so fast, you won't have time to collect your pink slip." Patricia's slick red lips, pasted in a fake smile, masked the menace of her tone.

With effort, Chloe held her temper in check. She would not be goaded into making a scene. "I'm a temporary teacher's aide. I'm not worried about a pink slip. Excuse me. I need to check on the refreshments." She headed to the kitchen, hoping to regain her equilibrium with some ginger ale.

Matt intercepted her, his eyes wide with worry. "Miss Martin. Have you seen Lindsay?"

"I saw her a while ago. Why?"

"Her friends say she went to the restroom but never came back. They checked, and she's not in there. We don't know where she went." His voice rose with each sentence.

She laid a reassuring hand on his shoulder. "Calm down, honey. I'm sure she's fine." Her rapid pulse rate belied her soothing words. "Let's take a look outside. Maybe she went to get some air." *Maybe she found Dylan.*

As they crossed the room, Daphne and Ellen joined them. Chloe pushed through the door, the kids trailing after her. A blast of cold air took her breath away. The thin silk of her dress did nothing to shield her from the elements. She should've grabbed her coat. Several kids stood huddled together in the parking lot, probably sharing a cigarette, but Lindsay was not among them.

"She's not answering her calls or texts, and she never does that." Fear made Daphne's eyes huge. "Something's happened to her, miss. I just know it."

"Do you know something we don't?"

"Right before she went to the restroom, Lindsay got a text from someone and she started acting funny. Wouldn't let any of us come with her to the bathroom. Said she wanted to be alone."

Chloe wrapped her arms around her middle, trying to keep warm. Maybe Lindsay felt sick and didn't want her friends to suspect she was pregnant.

"When she didn't come back, we went to find her, but the bathroom was empty," Ellen added. "We couldn't see her anywhere."

Goose bumps chased over Chloe's arms. "Let's go back and get our coats and start looking for her."

Matt appeared from the back of the building, holding something. "It's Lindsay's shoe, miss."

Dread froze Chloe's tracks. No way would the girl be walking around with one high-heeled shoe.

Matt's phone chimed. His eyes widened as he read the screen and the color drained from his already pale face. "They've got Lindsay."

27

Chloe was nowhere in sight.

A niggling sense of unease pricked at Aidan.

The front door opened on a cold gust of wind, and Chloe rushed in, followed by Matt, Daphne, and Ellen.

What were they doing outside with no coats? He headed to meet them, unease morphing into flat-out discomfort at the panicked look on their faces. "What's the matter?"

Chloe clutched his sleeve with near-frozen fingers. "It's Lindsay. She's missing. We think someone may have taken her."

Matt seemed ready to explode. "Sir, we need to find her. I don't know what they'll do to her."

Adrenaline pumped through Aidan's veins. "Give me a minute to tell the others." He found the custodian and one of the chaperones and gave them the necessary instructions. Then he grabbed his coat and joined Chloe and the kids.

"Matt, you'll come with me and Miss Martin. Girls, you need to stay inside until your ride comes to get you."

"But, sir—"

"No buts. We'll let you know as soon as we find her."

The two girls hugged each other as Aidan shepherded Matt and Chloe out the door.

"Call Chief Hiller. Tell him Lindsay is missing,"

Aidan said as they buckled up.

"No!" Panic laced Matt's voice. "They said they'd hurt her if we call the police."

Aidan glanced in the rearview mirror, relenting at the terror in Matt's eyes. "OK, we'll hold off for now." He fully intended to place a discreet call as soon as possible. "Where do you suggest we begin?"

"There's this place we used to meet. They might take her there."

"I'll need directions."

Bundled in her overcoat, Chloe sat stiff and silent in the passenger seat. Her lips, tinged with blue, trembled.

Aidan longed to envelop her in a hug and warm her with his body heat. Instead, he flicked the car heater to full blast. A dismal alternative. "We'll find her. Don't worry."

Aidan followed Matt's directions to the outskirts of town. He'd sent Mike Hillier a discreet text message, but tension built in Aidan's chest. He hoped Mike would come in an unmarked car to find them—the sooner the better.

Matt's directions led them to an industrial area on the outskirts of town.

"Stop here," Matt said sharply.

Aidan pulled up in front of an abandoned building. Grotesque graffiti covered the bricks, and broken glass cast jagged shadows over the ground.

"You hung out here?"

"Sometimes."

Aidan held back a derogatory comment. "Matt, you come with me. Chloe, keep the car doors locked and if we're not back in ten minutes, call the police."

"I'm coming with you." She went to open the

door, but he clamped a hand on her arm.

"It's too dangerous." He pinned her with a stern glare. "I'm bringing Matt because he knows his way around. If we find Lindsay, I'll call you."

A jumble of emotions crossed her features. "Fine. But be careful. Please."

Conscious of Matt in the back seat, Aidan checked the strong urge to kiss her. "We will. Remember, ten minutes. Then call the chief." He ignored Matt's sputter of protest. Aidan got out of the car, sidestepping litter and broken bottles. The stench of urine and stale liquor assailed his senses.

For all his bravado, Matt hugged Aidan's back as they made their way down a dark alley.

A silent prayer moved over Aidan's lips. *Please, Lord, keep us safe and help us find Lindsay before any harm comes to her.*

They entered the building through a side door.

"Down the hall on your right." Matt's whisper seemed loud in the cavernous area.

They inched forward in the blackness until a street lamp filtered through the broken windows, illuminating their way.

Matt pointed to a partly open door.

Noises from inside the room made the hairs rise on the back of Aidan's neck. He looked around for a weapon. The only viable item was a plank of wood. He picked it up, and then motioned for Matt to follow. Aidan moved through the doorway into a huge room, and his hope to go unnoticed evaporated.

Three dark figures whirled around.

Tension cinched Aidan's muscles. With sudden clarity, he realized how foolish he'd been to come here with only a teen for back up. He prayed Chloe would call Chief Hillier sooner rather than later. Better yet, that Mike was already en route.

"Where's my sister?" Anger laced Matt's voice.

One of the biggest guys strutted forward. The dark hood of his sweatshirt covered his head. "If it isn't my boy, Matt."

Aidan took a protective step forward. "Just give us the girl and we'll forget this ever happened."

The leader barked out a loud laugh. His cohorts joined in. "Why would we do that?"

The two others moved forward, revealing a figure on the floor behind them.

"What did you do to her?" The feral snarl erupted from Matt as he sprinted forward.

"Matt, no."

The boy dove at the leader, butting his head into the guy's stomach. The two hit the ground with a sickening thud.

When the others rushed forward, Aidan had no choice but to fend them off. Swinging the board, he connected with one kid's shoulder, knocking him over. Aidan's arm throbbed from the contact, but he regained his balance.

Matt was pinned under the leader.

Aidan wielded his weapon again, knocking the thug off Matt.

The other two rose and attacked as one.

Searing heat exploded across Aidan's shoulders. He let out a warlike yell and swung with all his strength, clipping one in the head.

Matt clung to another guy's back, choking him from behind.

The leader staggered to his feet and pulled a knife from his pant leg.

The air seized in Aidan's lungs. *God help us.* Would Chloe have called Mike yet? As the knife loomed closer, Aidan feared it wouldn't matter.

Chief Hillier would be much too late.

28

The siren's wail split the night.

Chloe released a pent up breath. *Thank you, God.* It had been ten minutes since Aidan and Matt had entered the building. She'd called the chief as soon as they'd gone in. But Aidan and Matt hadn't returned, and Chloe feared the worst.

When the police cruiser pulled up behind Aidan's car, Chloe jumped out onto the filthy sidewalk.

Chief Hillier met her, with a fresh-faced deputy trailing behind.

"Thanks for coming so quick." She pointed to the alley. "They went in through that side door."

"Joe and I will check it out." Mike motioned for the deputy to follow him.

Chloe stood on the sidewalk, her emotions shredded. She couldn't bear the thought of a possibly traumatized Lindsay being alone with gang members, or of Matt or Aidan being hurt. Ignoring her thudding heart, she entered the building.

Immediate blackness enveloped her, swallowing her whole. Perspiration dripped down her spine as she flattened her back to the wall and tried valiantly to control her fear. A scream sent chills down her arms. *Dear God, help us.*

"Stop. Police." Mike Hillier's voice boomed out.

Chloe snapped away from the wall to a nearby doorway and peered around the frame. Terror clouded her vision as she searched for Aidan in the melee.

Mike had one man pinned against the wall. Chloe made out two dark figures at the end of the room, but her focus snapped to the body on the ground. Her heart froze.

Aidan!

Joe held the radio to his mouth. "We need an ambulance at the abandoned warehouse on Thirty-Second Street."

Chloe's knees almost buckled as she rushed to Aidan's side. He lay very still, his eyes closed. Kneeling, Joe pressed his hand to Aidan's shoulder, but blood continued to seep through, soaking his shirt and jacket.

A sob rose in Chloe's throat. She picked up his cold hand. "Hang on, Aidan. The ambulance is coming."

Sounds of distress came from behind her. Chloe turned to see Matt hunched over Lindsay on the ground. Dark patches of blood stained the girl's dress.

Chloe dragged herself away from Aidan.

"Help her, Miss Martin. She's dying." Tears coursed down Matt's face.

Lindsay's lip was split, and bruises had begun to bloom on her cheek. The neckline of her dress was in ragged tatters. More bruises marred the whiteness of her arms.

From where the blood was situated on Lindsay's dress, Chloe had a pretty good idea of the cause.

Hot anger surged through her. What had Lindsay done to deserve this? Hadn't she been through enough misery in her short life?

She brushed a hand over the girl's hair. "Hang on, honey. We're here now, and no one's going to hurt you again."

~*~

Chloe's back ached from sitting on the hard plastic chair in the hospital waiting room. The overhead lights blinked and buzzed in annoying spurts. She pushed the hair off her face, fighting the fear that threatened to consume her. If someone didn't come out to tell her something—anything—about Aidan or Lindsay, she would storm the cubicles.

Beside her, Matt sat with his head hunched over his knees.

She placed a tentative hand on his back. "I'm sorry Lindsay didn't tell you about the baby. She didn't want anyone to know."

A tremor went through him.

"I want to kill Dylan Moore. And those animals—"

"It won't help Lindsay if you get into more trouble," Chloe said gently. "She needs you to be strong now."

Matt swiped an arm over his face and turned away.

"The best thing you can do for her is testify against the guy Chief Hillier caught. With your word, the chief's, and Mr. North's, he'll go to jail for sure. He might even be persuaded to turn in his friends."

Matt lifted terror-filled eyes to her. "The others will kill me," he whispered. "Why do you think I didn't get out long ago?" A look of complete hopelessness settled over his features.

She laid a hand on his arm. "You're not alone. You have all of us behind you."

A doctor clad in green scrubs entered the waiting

area. "Miss Martin?"

Chloe shot up. "Yes."

"Mr. North would like to see you now."

"Will he be OK?" She gripped her hands together to control the trembling.

"I believe so. He has a pretty nasty stab wound, but we've stitched him up. As long as he takes it easy for the next few weeks, he should be fine."

Relief flooded her body, leaving her weak. *Thank you, God.*

"How's my sister?" Matt asked.

"Another doctor is with her. You'll have to wait until he comes out."

Matt shoved his fists into his pocket and slumped back in his chair.

"Will you be OK for a few minutes while I check on Mr. North?" Chloe asked.

"Yeah."

"I won't be long." She followed the doctor past several curtained areas.

He pointed at a cubicle. "We'll be moving him to a room shortly, but you can go on in."

"Thank you."

Aidan lay completely still on the bed, his face as pale as the sheet covering him. Bulky bandages swathed his shoulder area, and one arm lay limply on top of the blanket.

He could have died tonight. Her throat tightened, and tears stung her eyes. Chloe raised a trembling hand to brush the hair off his forehead.

His eyes opened, and a faint smile bloomed. "Hi, beautiful." His voice rasped out in a hoarse whisper.

"Hi." A tear slid down her face. "How are you feeling?"

"Not bad. I think the drugs are working wonders." He nodded his head toward the IV pole. Behind it, monitors blinked.

"Can I get you anything? Water? Ice?"

"Nope. Having you here is all I need."

"That's all I need, too. To know you're OK." More tears blurred her vision. "When I saw you on that floor, I thought you were dead." Her world had almost crashed around her.

Aidan lifted his good arm and placed his palm against her cheek. "I'm alive, thanks to you. You called the chief right when I asked."

"Actually, I called him the minute you went in."

He gave a short laugh, and then winced. "I should've known." His breathing grew shallow. "How's Lindsay?"

"We're waiting for news. The doctor's still with her." Now was not the time to tell him everything.

"Did—did they catch them?" The effort to talk seemed to drain him of energy.

"They got one guy. Mike is hoping he'll give up the names of the others."

Aidan's lids began to droop.

"You should rest. Save your strength."

He opened his mouth to speak, but she silenced him with a quick kiss. "I'll be back after I check on Lindsay. You sleep now."

He mumbled something before his eyelids fluttered closed.

As Chloe stepped away from the bed, she thought she heard him say, "I love you, Chloe."

~*~

Chloe leaned against the wall in the corridor, her heart thundering an uneven beat. Had Aidan really said he loved her? She took in a shaky breath and attempted to focus on the kids. Matt needed her strength and calming presence. She only prayed Lindsay's prognosis was as positive as Aidan's.

As soon as Chloe arrived in the waiting room, Matt stopped pacing the floor.

"Any news on Lindsay?" she asked.

He shook his head.

Anxiety built to a painful pressure. She looped an arm around his thin shoulders. "Come on. Let's talk to the nurse."

The plump woman at the desk gave Chloe a sympathetic smile. "The doctor will be out when he's finished. I'm afraid you'll have to wait a bit longer."

"Could someone at least get us an update?"

The nurse nodded. "I'll see what I can find out." A few seconds later, she returned. "Good news. You can see her now. I'll take you over." She led them down the hall, past Aidan's curtain to another cubicle.

The doctor came out as they arrived.

"How's my sister?" Matt asked, his voice anxious.

The gray-haired man gave him a sympathetic pat on the shoulder. "She's got some fairly serious injuries, but she should make a full recovery." He paused. "I'm sorry to tell you that she lost the baby. Miscarriages at this stage of pregnancy are common, especially after the trauma she endured."

Poor Lindsay. How would she handle this devastating news?

"The worst of her injuries are a broken arm and two broken ribs. We've set the arm and taped the ribs as best we could. The other lacerations and bruising we're treating with ice and painkillers."

"Can I see her?" Matt asked.

"Sure. Just try not to wake her. She needs the sleep right now."

Matt stepped into the cubicle.

Chloe turned back to the doctor. "Were you able to tell if..." She trailed off, unable to voice to her question.

He gave her a frank look. "Besides the miscarriage and broken bones, there was no other sign of trauma. She was beaten, nothing more."

"Thank you, doctor." Chloe exhaled deeply. *One thing to be grateful for.*

"Do you know if the girl's parents are on the way? We need her medical history as well as insurance information."

Chloe stiffened. "I've left a message for her mother. The father's out of the picture." She prayed Mrs. Brown would pick up her voice mail message and get to the hospital.

"Let me know when you hear from her."

"I will. Thank you so much for your help."

He gave a brisk nod.

Chloe pushed through the opening in the curtain.

Bruised and swollen, Lindsay barely resembled the girl who'd arrived at the party that night. Her broken arm lay on top of the covers, the pink cast giving a garish glow. IV tubes snaked down to her taped hand.

Matt's head lay on Lindsay's good arm. Quiet sobs shook his frame. "I'm so sorry, Linds. This is all my fault."

Chloe slid beside him and laid her hand on Matt's back. "It's not your fault, honey. You're not responsible for what they did."

His shoulders continued to shake.

Chloe pulled up a chair and prepared to share his vigil. "Come on, let's pray for Lindsay and Mr. North." As she took Matt's hand and prayed out loud, she offered a silent entreaty to God for Matt's deliverance from the guilt that haunted him.

29

The throbbing in Aidan's head paled in comparison to the heat that shot through his shoulder. He groaned and opened his eyes. The smell of antiseptic and cleaning supplies made his stomach roil. He tried to push up with his good arm, but fell back, panting, when pain seared him.

"Let me help you." A tall nurse pushed a button to raise the head of the bed and rearranged the pillows behind him. "How are you feeling this morning?"

His face ached, fire burned his throat, and his head spun in dizzying circles. "I could use another dose of pain meds."

"We'll give you something after I take your vitals." She recorded something on a chart at the end of the bed. "If you're up for it, you have a couple of visitors." She handed him a small cup with pills and some water.

Chloe. Anticipation had his pulse roaring. He took the meds in a daze, his mind moving to last night. Hazy memories of her hand on his forehead, her lips brushing his, flitted across his mind. Did he dream it? "Send them in."

Moments later, Maxi's elfin face appeared in the doorway. Her hazel eyes clouded with concern as she leaned over to kiss his cheek.

Aidan winced even at that feather touch and tried not to let his disappointment show.

"You gave us all a scare, mister. What were you thinking? Charging into that building with only a teenager for back-up?"

"I know. Dumb move." A sickening thought hit him. "Matt wasn't hurt, was he?"

"He's fine. And Lindsay has some bruises and broken bones, but she'll be OK."

Broken bones? An image flashed in his memory. The inert form of Lindsay on the warehouse floor, her dress covered in blood. Broken bones wouldn't have caused that.

A light knock drew his gaze across the room.

Chloe stepped inside. "Can you handle one more visitor?"

The pleasure of seeing her eclipsed his pain for the moment. "Sure. Come in."

She looked like an angel in a white frothy blouse with her hair caught in a loose ponytail at the nape of her neck. In the morning light, her eyes appeared almost golden. She moved in beside Maxi. "How are you feeling?"

"I'll feel a lot better when the pain meds kick in." As much as he loved his sister, he wished she would leave him alone with Chloe. He had a lot he wanted to tell her. Like his last thought before blacking out had been of her. And the one regret he'd had was that she'd never know he loved her. He planned to remedy that fact before the end of the day. Studying her, he noted her pinched features and the sadness in her eyes. "How's Lindsay?"

"She's stable. I'm going to see her after you."

"And Matt?"

"Physically, he's fine. But he's feeling incredibly guilty. I couldn't get him to leave Lindsay last night."

Their gazes locked. He longed to take her hand, but not with Maxi there. Instead he tried to convey comfort with his eyes.

Maxi cleared her throat. "Well, I'll leave you two alone. Don't wear the man out, Chlo." She leaned over to kiss him again. "When they let you out of here, Jason and I want you to come and stay with us. Mama's frantic, so I'll go over now and reassure her."

"Tell her I'm fine. And thanks for the offer. I might take you up on it."

"You *will* take us up on it." She shot Chloe a mischievous look. "Unless Chloe wants you all to herself." Chuckling, Maxi swept out of the room.

Chloe pulled a chair over. He reached through the metal bars and entwined his fingers with hers. "What's Lindsay's real condition? Everyone's been so vague."

"She has a broken arm, cracked ribs, and her face..." Chloe's voice wavered and she swallowed hard.

The air whooshed out of Aidan's lungs. Those animals had beaten her. If only he'd gotten there before the damage had been done.

Cool fingers touched his jaw. "You and Matt saved her life, Aidan. Be happy things weren't worse."

The raw emotion swirling in the golden depths of her eyes mirrored his own unsettled feelings. "I saw a lot of blood on her clothes. Was that from the beating?"

The fingers gripping the metal bar of his bed turned white. "Indirectly. Lindsay had a...miscarriage."

"Lindsay was pregnant?" His voice nearly failed him.

"Yes."

Realization slowly dawned. "You knew about

this?"

Misery shone in Chloe's eyes. She nodded.

"And you never told me?"

"Lindsay didn't want anyone to know. Not even Matt."

"You had a responsibility, Chloe. Did you at least make sure her mother knew?"

"I did." She wouldn't meet his gaze.

Warning bells rang in his head. Before he could question her further, a knock broke the silence.

Chief Hillier entered the room, his expression grim. "Sorry to interrupt, but I need to talk to both of you."

"Come in, Mike."

The chief pulled out a small notepad and pencil. "I guess you heard we have one of the perpetrators from last night in custody. So far he's not saying much. I took Chloe's statement, but I need your version of what happened."

Quickly, Aidan relayed the events of the previous evening.

When he finished, Mike looked up. "What can you tell me about these alleged gang members?"

"Not much. It was dark and they were wearing hoods."

"Matt Brown knows more than what he's saying. I want to lean on him a little more, but I'll need to talk to his mother first. To make sure she's OK with it." Mike turned his steely gaze to Chloe. "That's where you come in."

The color drained from Chloe's face. "I—I don't understand."

"I believe you've been in recent contact with Mrs. Brown. In the Lucky Times Tavern."

~*~

How could Chief Hillier know about that? Chloe licked her dry lips, trying desperately to come up with a suitable answer. "Could we talk outside? I don't want to tire Aidan."

"Actually, I'd like to hear the answer." Aidan's suspicious gaze shot to her.

Chief Hillier watched her with unflappable calm.

Short of fainting on the spot, she could see no way out of this. *Lord, give me the words to make them understand*. She squared her shoulders. "Yes, I've spoken with Mrs. Brown."

"So you were aware the Brown kids were living on their own for months now in decrepit conditions?"

Chloe felt the noose tightening around her neck. "Yes," she whispered.

The only sound in the room was the whir of machines monitoring Aidan's vital signs.

"May I ask why you failed to report this to anyone?" Mike's scowling demeanor did not give Chloe much hope of sympathy.

"I...I didn't want Matt and Lindsay to be forced into foster care. Not with Matt's gang connections."

"Is that why you asked Mrs. Brown to let the kids to move in with you?"

"What?" The disbelief in Aidan's voice sent chills of regret down her spine.

Mike was toying with her. Obviously he'd spoken with Mrs. Brown if he knew all of this. "I'm sure Mrs. Brown told you it's a temporary measure until she can find a job in Rainbow Falls."

"I take it you knew nothing about this?" Mike

asked Aidan.

Aidan's face seemed chiseled from rock. "No."

Chloe hated the coldness in his voice, the return of his anger and disdain.

Mike snapped his notebook closed. "I could charge you with child endangerment, you know."

Chloe bit back a gasp. "But I was only trying to protect them."

"That's not how it looks from where I stand. Did you also know about Lindsay Brown's pregnancy?" His steely eyes pierced hers with no hint of softening. The fact that Mike was Nick's best friend wouldn't help her today.

"Yes." How had this all gone so terribly wrong? She'd wanted to help Lindsay and Matt, not bring more trouble to their lives.

"Miss Martin, I'm afraid you'll have to come with me for further questioning."

30

In the space of twenty-four hours, Aidan's world had turned upside down. He'd chased an abducted student, gotten stabbed and almost died, and discovered the woman he loved had been deceiving him for weeks.

A teenage pregnancy and a mother virtually abandoning her kids. How had these details escaped his notice? Tension tightened his neck muscles, the ugly truth bringing with it a measure of guilt. When Matt had gotten into trouble, Aidan had been suspicious that Mrs. Brown wasn't there, but he'd ignored the warning signs.

Still, Chloe had no right to keep something of this magnitude from him.

Another conversation filtered through his memory. *"What happens if we find out there's no mother living there?"*

"I'd be forced to call the county social services and report neglect. They'd probably put Matt into foster care."

Had she known even then that Mrs. Brown was living elsewhere? Why hadn't she trusted him enough to ask for his help? Did she think him so unfeeling that he could turn the kids over to the county without a thought?

Aidan rubbed a hand over the ache in his chest, an ache that had nothing to do with his stab wound. He'd planned to reveal his feelings for Chloe today. Good thing Chief Hillier got there first. His head flopped onto the pillow. Searing agony ripped through his shoulder, stealing his breath, yet the emotional pain was worse.

A knock at the door forced his eyes open.

Larry Jenkins stood in the doorway. "You look terrible." He removed his fedora and shuffled in.

"Being stabbed will do that to you."

Larry remained serious, sending another warning to Aidan's pain-addled mind. "Grab a seat."

"I don't think I'll be here long. I have some unpleasant business to discuss."

"Bad news travels fast in this town."

"I'm afraid it does. This is one devil of a mess." Furrows creased his forehead. "In light of recent events involving Matt and Lindsay Brown, I have no choice but to suspend you from your position as Vice-Principal."

"You can't be serious."

"I'm afraid so. Too many rules have been breached, by you and Miss Martin." He gave a weary sigh. "There will be a hearing in due course."

A cold swath of dread swirled through Aidan's system. It was Arizona all over again. "Larry, you can't do this."

"I'm sorry. I have no choice." He pushed his fedora back on and walked out the door, his shoulders hunched.

Acid burned in Aidan's stomach. He never should have gotten involved with Chloe Martin. She'd been trouble from the moment she'd crashed through his front door. Now his life, his heart, and his career lay in ruins. How would he ever recover this time?

~*~

Chloe poured a cup of strong, black coffee. She grimaced at her rumpled sweats and wrinkled T-shirt. Cinderella was indeed back from the ball. She'd been so exhausted when the chief had finally released her that she'd come home and fallen into bed, grateful for the oblivion of sleep.

At least Mike wasn't going to press charges—for now.

Chloe needed to work fast, however, to get things into motion for the Brown kids before Mike sent Matt to foster care. After a fitful night, she was finding it hard to muster the energy to do anything. Her mind kept swirling back to the look of utter devastation on Aidan's face. As soon as visiting hours began, she'd go talk to him. If she could only make him understand why she couldn't tell him about Mrs. Brown, surely he'd find it in his heart to forgive her—again.

A loud rap banged on her door.

When she opened the locks, Maxi's anxious face greeted her.

"Hi. I don't have long. I've come to pick up some of Aidan's things, but I had to talk to you."

"What's the matter? Has something else happened?"

Maxi pushed past her into the living room. "I guess you haven't heard. Principal Jenkins suspended Aidan."

Chloe gasped. "Why did he do that?"

Maxi threw out her arms while she paced. "Aidan wouldn't tell me everything. It has something to do with those kids. It also has something to do with you. I tried to pry it out of him, but he clammed right up."

"This is terrible. I have to talk to him."

"I'm supposed to pick him up after I get his stuff. Why don't you go see him now? I'll stall as long as I can."

Chloe made the trip to Kingsville in record time. Nerves wreaked havoc with her system as she raced up to the second floor, not bothering to wait for the elevator. Outside Aidan's room, she paused to catch her breath and collect her thoughts. *Lord, give me the words to convince Aidan how sorry I am. Help him see that we can get through this crisis together.*

Seated on the side of the bed, one arm in a sling, Aidan's head snapped up as she entered. A shuttered look came over his features, and he turned away.

Chloe fought back a rush of dismay. "I need to talk to you about what happened yesterday."

"Mike made the situation pretty clear."

His harsh tone tore into her.

"I want to explain."

He turned to face her, his features as rigid as a mask. "What's to explain? You lied to me. And almost got Lindsay, Matt, and I killed. I don't need to hear anything else."

His coldness penetrated her hollow insides, creating tremors that shook her to the core. "I didn't want you to send Matt into foster care."

Anger leapt into his eyes, turning them to molten steel. "Who were you to make that decision on your own?"

Chloe cringed. She'd made a huge mess of everyone's lives. Now Aidan could lose his job. A job that meant everything to him. "I'm so sorry, Aidan. I never thought—"

"Save it, Chloe. Your apologies can't fix this."

"I'm sorry," she repeated as tears burned her eyes. "So very sorry."

"I think you'd better go." He stared at the wall, a nerve ticking in his jaw.

Before she lost complete control, she rushed from the room.

~*~

After a visit to the women's restroom where she splashed cold water on her face and attempted to collect her tattered emotions, Chloe made her way to Lindsay's room. She needed to have a serious talk with the kids. She owed Lindsay and Matt an apology. She'd thought she could handle the situation, but she'd only made everything worse.

The sheets covered Lindsay's still form as she slept. One side of her face had turned purple and her lip was swollen. Chloe forced herself to face what this girl had suffered, before shifting her attention to Matt, who sat curled in one of the chairs, asleep with his head on the wooden armrest. From the looks of it, he'd been here the whole time.

Lindsay's eye fluttered open as Chloe approached the bed.

"Hey, honey. How are you feeling?"

Lindsay opened cracked lips. "Sore."

"Do you want me to get the nurse?"

"No. Just want water."

Chloe picked up a cup and angled the straw towards Lindsay's lips.

The girl took a few sips, and then dropped her head back onto the pillow.

What could Chloe say to a girl who'd been

through such an ordeal? She laid a gentle hand on her hair. "I know it doesn't feel like it now, but the doctor says you'll be fine."

Tears welled in Lindsay's eyes. "My…my baby's gone."

Chloe reached to grasp her hand. "I'm so sorry, honey." *How many times would she utter those inadequate words today?*

The girl's body convulsed with sobs.

Chloe handed her a tissue, wishing she could do more to comfort the girl.

When at last the crying subsided, Lindsay took in a shaky breath. "Where's Matt? Is he OK?"

"He's right here. Asleep on the chair. He hasn't left your side for a minute."

"Thank God." She let out a long breath. "How will we keep him safe?"

"Actually I want to talk to you both about that." Chloe turned to rouse Matt who stirred in the chair. "Matt, I need to talk to you and Lindsay about something important."

He rubbed his eyes, pushed his tousled hair off his forehead, and straightened.

In quick terms, she told them of her plan. "Moving in would be a temporary solution, until your mother gets a better job in town."

The lines of worry in Lindsay's forehead relaxed. "I don't know about Matt, but I'd like that."

"What do you think, Matt? We'd have to draw up some rules, so there won't be any misunderstandings between us."

Matt remained silent.

"The only other option is foster care. Now that Chief Hillier knows your circumstances, he's already setting those wheels in motion."

Matt's head snapped up, alarm lighting his eyes.

"I'm hoping that with your mother's permission, he'll let you stay with me." She put a gentle hand on his arm and waited until he looked at her. "I care about you and Lindsay very much. And I'll do whatever it takes to keep you both safe—if you'll let me."

Only the trembling of his bottom lip gave away any emotion. At last, he swiped his sleeve under his nose and nodded.

With that one small gesture, a new alliance was forged.

31

Monday morning dawned cold and gray with a torrent of sleet descending on the town. The bleakness of the sky matched the state of Chloe's heart. Still, she dressed with purpose, digging deep to find her determination. Today she would plead her case before Mr. Jenkins. She needed to take responsibility for the events that had transpired and prayed that she could persuade the principal not to fire Aidan.

Chloe arrived at the school an hour before classes began and made her way toward Mr. Jenkins' office. When she reached Aidan's darkened room, she laid her palm against the door and absorbed a wave of sorrow. He should be sitting at his desk right now, getting a head start on the day, not recovering from a stab wound. Chloe's well-meaning but reckless actions had led to this—to Aidan being forced to leave the job he loved. With renewed purpose, she straightened her spine. If all went well with Mr. Jenkins, justice would be restored, and Aidan would be back where he belonged.

The door to the principal's office stood ajar.

Nerves slicked Chloe's palms with sweat. She offered a quick prayer for guidance before knocking.

"Come in." Mr. Jenkins sat at a desk piled with papers and used coffee mugs. Unsmiling, the man gestured to a chair. "Have a seat, Miss Martin."

"Thank you for agreeing to see me."

"I was going to call you anyway. You saved me the trouble."

She nodded, trying not to let his scowl get the best of her. "First of all, I want to apologize for everything that's happened. Despite my good intentions, I can see now how many errors in judgment I made along the way."

"That's an understatement. You've created a terrible predicament for Mr. North."

Unwanted tears clogged Chloe's throat. She'd sworn she wouldn't break down. "That's the reason I'm here. I want to emphasize that Mr. North is innocent in all of this. He had no idea Mrs. Brown wasn't living with her children, or that Lindsay was pregnant. I kept this information from him because I knew he'd be required to report it to the appropriate authorities."

"And why exactly were you so opposed to that? I think a good foster home would be a better option than their present situation."

She met his gaze. "I felt it would be harmful to Matt. He's been abandoned by his father, and his mother as well. He has a lot of misplaced anger, which, frankly, I feel foster care would only magnify."

"And you're an expert in this field? A twenty-three-year old with a culinary degree?"

"No, sir. I'm not an expert. But I do know a lot about bad choices and the devastation they can cause. I was trying to save two kids from the same mistakes I've made, or worse."

He studied her. "I'll accept that your intentions were good. However, your naiveté has led to devastating consequences."

She lifted her chin. "I'm willing to take full

responsibility for my mistakes, but Mr. North should not be blamed for things he knew nothing about. He is an honest, principled man, who wouldn't break the rules for anything."

"Really?" Mr. Jenkins elbowed a pile of papers out of the way and leaned in, his eyes hard. "Then maybe you can clear up another rumor circulating around the school."

Acid burned in the pit of her stomach. "What rumor?"

"I've been told that you and Mr. North are romantically involved. Is this true?"

Every drop of saliva seemed to disappear, gluing her tongue to the roof of her mouth. How could she answer this question without incriminating Aidan? "I can't deny I've come to develop…feelings…for Mr. North, but we are definitely not a couple." Pain squeezed her heart at this admission.

"You danced around that question better than a politician. Are you romantically involved with him?"

The temptation to lie to save Aidan's job burned bright. But lies had created this mess in the first place. "We have kissed," she admitted. "But Aidan made it clear there would be no relationship."

"A teacher reported seeing you two locked in a passionate embrace the other night at the youth center opening."

Anger pumped hard in her chest. "That is an outright lie. Whoever said that has her own agenda for spreading such gossip."

"You have to understand how bad this looks for Aidan, considering he was let go from his last position."

Outraged, Chloe shot to her feet. "Mr. Jenkins, you

know Aidan. He is the most honorable, upright man I have ever met. The only mistake he made was trying to help a student...and getting involved with the wrong woman." The irony of that statement made her pause. "And now he holds himself back, afraid to care too much, in case his actions are misinterpreted." She realized then how much it had cost Aidan to go after Lindsay. His sacrifice humbled her. "Aidan put his own safety in jeopardy to save Lindsay from those thugs. Punishing him for that would be the worst type of injustice."

"I can see you feel strongly about this."

"Yes, sir, I do. And just as strongly about Matt and Lindsay. I can't allow them to be put into foster care. Mrs. Brown has agreed to let the kids move in with me until she can find a job in town."

"Well, that's one matter I have no control over. I do, however, have the power, and the duty, to relieve you of your work here."

She nodded. "I understand. But please, please reconsider Mr. North's position. You'll never find a more dedicated, caring person. His career means everything to him."

"I appreciate your views on the matter, Miss Martin. All I can say is that I will take them into consideration." Mr. Jenkins pushed up from his chair, signaling her time was up.

"Thank you. Now if you'll excuse me, I'll collect my things."

~*~

A week after Aidan was released, he stopped in the corridor outside his darkened office and waited for the rush of regret to subside. What would he do if he were forced to leave this job where he'd felt such a sense of fulfillment? Here, everyone knew his family and his history. With the whole town as witnesses, his downfall would be all the more painful. Since leaving the hospital, Aidan's physical pain had subsided, but the sting of Chloe's betrayal burned worse than the knife wound in his shoulder.

He fought down his negativity and continued on to the conference room.

Larry had called this meeting of the superintendent, two other board officials, and himself.

Today he would learn the fate of his career. While he'd been recuperating, a hearing had occurred. He'd been allowed to send a written statement in his defense but hadn't heard anything back, and he was totally unprepared for the final decision. He'd prayed all week that the truth would become evident, and he would be allowed to return. If not, he had no idea what he would do with the rest of his life. He took a seat in one of the chairs surrounding the large, oval conference table and bowed his head in one last fervent prayer. *Please help me to accept Your will, Lord, whatever the board decides. I trust in Your plan for my life.*

Voices echoed in the outer hall, and Larry entered, followed by three other men. They shook hands and took their spots around the table with Larry at the head.

"Thank you for coming, gentlemen. Mr. North and I appreciate your counsel in this matter."

The men murmured their response.

"Let's get right to it. I understand you've reached a decision."

The superintendent, Mr. Walters, nodded. "We

have." He turned his gaze to Aidan. "Mr. North, after careful consideration of all testimonies, including your written one, we have determined that you were unaware of the events surrounding the Brown children. We have decided to overlook the ill-advised actions, which led to your stabbing, and have ruled that you should not be held responsible for Miss Martin's misconduct."

Misconduct? That seemed a bit harsh. Though misguided, Chloe's motives were well-intended.

"You are hereby re-instated to the position of Vice-Principal and will be reimbursed for your brief time of suspension."

A wave of relief spread through his body, leaving him lightheaded. "Thank you, sir. I appreciate your faith in me."

Larry smiled. "Actually you owe a lot to Miss Martin. I've never heard such a staunch defense of character as the one she gave on your behalf, both to me privately, and at the hearing."

Mr. Walters nodded. "A very passionate, albeit naïve, young woman. You're lucky to have her on your side."

Aidan blinked, trying to process how they could condemn Chloe one minute and sing her praises the next. And luck had nothing to do with her testimony. He sent silent thanks to God.

The superintendent and his associates shook hands, and then left the room.

Larry remained at the table, collecting his papers.

On his way out, Aidan paused. "Larry, I have to ask…What exactly did Chloe tell you?"

Larry's brows rose. "Let's just say, I almost had to put on my sunglasses for the glow of the halo she painted over your head."

Chloe had defended him?

Aidan swallowed the emotion lodged in his throat. "I guess I'll see you next week then. The doctor says I need a few more days before going back to work."

"Take your time. Your job will be here when you're ready."

Aidan thanked him and walked out. Chloe's testimony on his behalf warmed the cold places in his heart—places that had frozen over the night Chief Hillier had questioned her in the hospital. He couldn't help but compare Patricia's lack of loyalty at a time of crisis to Chloe's staunch defense, even after he'd coldly rejected her apology. Thanks to her endorsement, he had his job back.

She'd put his welfare above her own, hadn't even tried to save herself. Nor had she used Aidan's position to justify her actions. Deep down, Chloe was a good person. He just wished he could trust her enough to risk his heart.

Too many deceptions—too many secrets—made that impossible.

32

Three months later

A blast of cold March air whipped through the front door of *Chloe's Confections*.

Chloe grinned as Lindsay entered, book bag over her shoulder. "Hi, honey. How was school?"

Lindsay stamped her feet and brushed the snow from her shoulders. "Good. I sent in my college applications today. The guidance teacher helped me do it electronically."

"That's wonderful." Chloe leaned over the counter to see Lindsay better. "So have you given any more thought to entering the Junior Chef competition?"

Lindsay removed her bag and coat and hung them on the rack. She turned to face Chloe with a hesitant smile. "I think I'd like to try—if you'll help me."

A rare burst of joy spread through Chloe's chest. "Of course I'll help. This competition will be a great experience for you."

Lindsay grabbed an apron from the hook and tied it around her waist. "Working here has been great too. I've learned so much from you already."

After three months in business, *Chloe's Confections* continued to flourish. In addition to Matt and Lindsay, who worked part-time after school and on weekends, Chloe had been able to hire more staff, enabling her to spend the bulk of her time in the kitchen where she was happiest.

Chloe helped Lindsay clear the dishes left from a late lunch crowd. If business kept up, she'd have to consider expanding the eating area. Excitement rushed through her veins at the thought.

Over the past few months, the bakery had become Chloe's salvation. Throwing all her energy into her business allowed her to block out the pain of Aidan's rejection—most of the time. She still couldn't walk through the front door of her apartment without a sharp jab to her heart.

Aidan had moved out soon after he recovered from the stabbing. He obviously couldn't stand to be around her. His move made that abundantly clear.

For now, she worked to make up for her mistakes with Matt and Lindsay. "I'm glad you like it here. But the truth is you've helped me far more than I helped you. I could never have made it through these last few months without you."

The Browns' old apartment had needed major repairs, and the landlord had actually stepped up to get them done. Mrs. Brown had given permission for Matt and Lindsay to move in with Chloe temporarily, a huge blessing which had provided Chloe with the sense of family she'd always longed for, and given the kids a sense of stability they'd lacked.

Chloe thanked God every day for the way Lindsay and Matt had blossomed.

After several weeks of melancholy over the loss of her baby, Lindsay had come to terms with it, and now focused her energy on the future.

Matt had finally agreed to testify against the gang members, and the leader had been sent to jail, effectively disbanding the group. Without that threat hanging over his head, Matt's marks had improved at school, and he now enjoyed a new circle of friends.

Lindsay paused in mid-swipe of one of the tables. "You've done so much for us. I don't know how we'll ever pay you back."

Chloe swallowed a rush of emotion. "Just be happy. That's all the thanks I need."

Lindsay gave a sad smile. "I wish you could be happy too. If only Mr. North—"

The front door flew open, saving Chloe from the torment of that unfinished thought.

Matt rushed in with a flurry of snowflakes, a grin splitting his face. "Linds, guess what?" He waved his phone. "Mom just called. She got that job, and she's looking for a better apartment in town."

As Lindsay whooped with delight and rushed to hug her brother, Chloe's hands stilled. She'd known the day would come when Mrs. Brown would return, but foolishly she'd hoped they could go on this way indefinitely.

"Too bad Mr. North's old apartment is rented." Lindsay glanced over at Chloe. "It would've been perfect. We could've come upstairs and visited any time we wanted."

Chloe swallowed the tears that threatened to choke her and nodded.

"I wish Mr. North would take you back. Then you wouldn't be alone when we leave."

Matt snorted. "That's not gonna happen. He's got a girlfriend."

A mug slipped from Chloe's fingers and crashed to the floor, splintering into fragments.

Lindsay rushed over to help, eyes swimming with sympathy. "It's Miss Peters. She teaches at the elementary school now."

A dark cloud filled Chloe's soul as she swept up the broken slivers. She hated to see Aidan with a woman who didn't share his faith or his moral values. He deserved so much better.

Chloe rose and deposited the debris into the trash can, staring at the jagged shards. Much like her shattered heart, there was no putting those pieces back together again.

~*~

Aidan walked into Maxi's kitchen and sniffed in appreciation of the apple pie she must have baking in the oven. "Hey, sis. What's so urgent I had to leave work early?"

She'd left a message on his voice mail at work, demanding he come out to the farmhouse as soon as possible.

Maxi turned off the tap and dried her hands. "Thanks for coming. Have a seat."

Aidan frowned, but remained standing, tension seizing his neck muscles. Maxi seemed on edge, not her usual bubbly self. "Is everything all right? Ben's not sick, is he?"

"Ben and Jason are fine."

Alarm spiked through him. "Is it Mom?"

"Mama's fine too."

"Then what's the problem?"

She took a seat at the table. "Please sit down. I don't need a crick in my neck."

He sat down across from her. "What is it?"

"I want to talk to you about Patricia. And don't roll your eyes at me."

Annoyance crept through his system. "There's

nothing to talk about. We're just friends."

"You might think so, but I guarantee you that woman is out to get a ring on her finger."

"That's not going to happen." Aidan couldn't totally discount his sister's observation. Patricia had been angling for a commitment since she'd moved to Rainbow Falls. Marriage, however, couldn't be farther from his mind. Not when he couldn't stop thinking about Chloe.

Even after all this time, he could still smell her hair when he closed his eyes. Loneliness had driven him to seek some type of companionship outside of his family. So he'd invited Patricia out for a few meals, making his stipulation of a platonic relationship clear from the outset.

Aidan's stomach rumbled, reminding him he'd skipped lunch. He pulled an apple from the fruit bowl on the table and took a bite, hoping Maxi would change the subject.

She pinned him with a hard look. "Isn't it time you talked to Chloe?"

Aidan sputtered. Juice dribbled down his chin while irritation shot up his spine. "I'm not discussing this with you again."

Maxi poked a finger in his chest. "What kind of Christian are you? How can you forgive Patricia and not Chloe?"

"I've forgiven Chloe. But I can't forget what she did."

"Yet you have no problem overlooking Patricia's actions."

He scrubbed a hand over his jaw. "I'm not romantically involved with her. I know exactly what type of person she is, and I accept that."

"Then why can't you accept Chloe? Why is she so different?"

Because I loved her, and she let me down. The selfish thought jarred him. With added energy, he bit hard into the apple.

"Chloe didn't set out to hurt you. She was following her heart—following her need to help those kids. She withheld information from you to protect you from the fallout. To make sure you wouldn't be implicated." Maxi jumped up, agitation evident in her jerky hand movements. "She's taken in those two teens and has done wonders with them. She volunteers at Nick's shelter for abused women. She's even helping Mrs. Brown find a job and an apartment."

Aidan's back muscles tensed into painful spasms. The wound in his shoulder throbbed an accompanying symphony. "I get it. She's a saint. What's your point?"

Maxi scowled, fury glowing in her hazel eyes. "My point is that your huge ego is keeping you from seeing the truth about a woman who loves you."

Aidan shot to his feet. "I don't have to listen to this."

"I hope your self-righteousness keeps you warm at night."

"That's enough, Maxine."

She crossed the floor to face him. "Why? Are you going to write me off too?"

Her stark words halted his retreat, freezing his feet to the floor. Is that how he came across? As self-righteous and condescending?

"You're so busy making sure everyone else is perfect, you don't take time to look at yourself. Probably because even *you* wouldn't measure up to your own impossible standards."

The truth rang hard in his ears as he slammed out of Maxi's screen door.

~*~

Aidan slipped into the back pew of the Good Shepherd Church on Sunday morning and ducked low in his seat. He'd avoided going to church lately, mostly because he couldn't bear to see Chloe sitting with Lily and the kids. It hurt too much.

After Maxi's dressing down, Aidan had been doing some hard thinking, and he wasn't proud of what he'd discovered. Unlike Chloe, who owned her mistakes and tried her best to make up for them, Aidan had worn his intolerance like a suit of armor, taking no blame at all for what had happened. When had he become so superior?

The organ sang out the first strains of the opening hymn.

Aidan opened a hymnbook. Today he planned to pray hard for God's forgiveness and by doing so, hoped he could learn to forgive himself.

A blur rushed by up the aisle, stirring the air around him. His heart thundered a response, moments before he even realized who it was.

His hungry eyes followed Chloe to the first pew.

A deep ache vibrated through his body, matching the sad tones of the organ. He rubbed his chest to relieve the building pressure. *How he missed her.* He'd moved out of his apartment because he couldn't bear seeing her every day, hearing her heels tap across the floor above him. No matter how hard he tried to hang onto his anger, he could only seem to remember her good qualities.

Nick approached the pulpit and began to preach. "I'll start my sermon today with a quote from Ephesians, chapter 4. 'Be kind to one another, tender-hearted, forgiving each other, just as God in Christ also has forgiven you.'

Tender-hearted. Forgiving. Shame burned in Aidan's stomach. What kind of Christian was he when he held grudges, showed no tolerance, and withheld his forgiveness like some treasured prize to be earned?

"It could be argued that a sin is a sin. Yet along with the black and white, there exists many shades of gray. No one is perfectly good or perfectly bad." Nick's eyes skimmed the congregation. "So let us be mindful of this as we strive for truth in our lives. Let us forgive others, and ourselves, if we slip up from time to time. Try not to judge another's misstep, lest your own be judged as well."

Nick's gaze seemed to pierce right through Aidan as the words sank in. *No one is perfectly good or perfectly bad.* That's exactly what Maxi had been trying to tell him the other day. He wasn't perfect, and he shouldn't expect everyone else to be. *Oh Lord, he'd been such a fool.* He'd allowed his pride to overshadow everything else, and by doing so, he had failed to see the bigger picture.

Not only had Chloe been trying to save the kids, but in her own way, she'd been protecting him too, preventing him from having to make the call that might ruin their lives.

And despite his harsh condemnation of her, she'd taken the full blame for the situation. Defended his good character and exonerated him completely. No one had ever done that for him before. How could he have been so blind?

At the end of the service, Aidan remained seated

until most of the congregation filed out of the building. He didn't see where Chloe had gone. Just as well. He needed time to figure out how he would apologize to her. And this time beg *her* forgiveness. Aidan sat with his eyes closed until he sensed someone standing in the aisle.

"Nice to see you back finally."

Aidan's eyes opened at Nick's deep voice.

Still dressed in his clerical collar and black shirt, his friend's eyes crinkled in a smile. "I hope this means you'll stop avoiding me too."

Guilt slid through Aidan's system. "Hey, Nick." He rose from the hard bench, casting furtive glances around the church.

"She's outside with Lily."

Aidan stiffened.

The smile faded from Nick's face. "If you'd just talk to her, I'm sure you could clear things up."

Aidan met Nick's gaze, his jaw tight. "I thought you didn't want me dating Chloe."

"I was wrong to interfere. Sometimes it's hard to remember that Chloe's a grown woman. She tries hard to hide it, but I know she's in a world of pain."

Aidan sucked in a sharp breath as his own agony stabbed the region around his heart.

"I only want Chloe to be happy, and I think you have the power to make that happen." Nick laid a hand on his shoulder. "Will you talk to her at least?"

A surge of hope leapt in Aidan's veins. "I'll definitely think about it."

33

Chloe hummed the tune to the last hymn as she parked in front of the bakery. She got out of the car and glanced at her watch. She must have just missed Dorothy.

Dorothy Brown volunteered for the Sunday shift so that Chloe was free to attend church. Chloe had hoped to catch her before she left to discuss next week's schedule. No matter, Chloe only needed to dash in and get the cake Maxi had ordered for Jason's surprise birthday luncheon. Designing the cake with a fire engine theme had been pure pleasure for Chloe. The look on Jason's face when he saw it would be the virtual icing on top. Chloe chuckled. Hard to predict who would like it more—Jason or little Ben. Like his father, the boy was obsessed with fire trucks.

Chloe was looking forward to the party. All her family and friends would be there. The one drawback would be seeing Aidan again. Chloe sighed, wondering if Maxi had told him she was coming. Probably not. Knowing the way Aidan felt about her, he likely wouldn't show.

She tried not to let sadness dim her good mood. *Lord, give me the strength to face Aidan, especially if he's with Patricia. Help me to withstand the pain and not ruin the celebration for my friends.*

She snapped on the lights and stopped to admire the sparkling room. A sigh of pure satisfaction escaped as she ran her fingers across the oversized, stainless steel refrigerator. With a hard tug, she pulled the door open.

Carefully, she lifted the cake out and set it on the counter. When the bell jangled out front, her heart somersaulted. Even after all this time, Chloe couldn't keep images of the assault from her mind. Shaking, she plucked a large knife out of the block, and then crouched to peer around the corner into the café.

Aidan?

She shot upright so fast that her feet slipped out from under her. With a thud, she landed on her rear, the knife clattering across the floor. Heat flooded her neck and cheeks. Would she ever stop making a fool of herself in front of him?

His shadow hovered over her. "Are you all right?"

"I'm fine." She scrambled to her knees on the cold tiles. "What are you doing here?"

A smile tugged at his lips as he held out a hand to assist her. "Maxi sent me to pick up the cake."

Frowning, Chloe pulled her hand free. "Why would she do that? She knew I was bringing it with me." She stifled a groan. "Oh, no. Looks like the matchmaker is at it again." She ducked back into the kitchen.

"I'm actually glad to have the chance to talk to you alone." He followed her in. "You've done a great job here, Chloe. The bakery is beautiful."

"Thank you." Her stomach did flips. She couldn't bear him being so close, and moved behind the worktable, where she pulled out a large cardboard box and began to pack up the cake.

Regret reflected in his gray eyes. "I owe you a long overdue apology. I reacted badly about the whole situation with Matt and Lindsay. I realize now that you were only trying to protect the kids—and me, as well. I'm just sorry it took me so long to figure that out."

His words should have brought her such joy, but wisps of sadness curled around her heart. "And I'm sorry I almost got you fired," she said quietly. "I hope you can forgive me for that."

"I'm the one who needs forgiveness. For harboring such anger and self-righteousness. I've been a real jerk."

A fierce defensiveness rose in her chest. "You're not a jerk. You're an upstanding person who demands the same of the people around him. There's nothing wrong with that."

A ghost of a smile hovered. "You make it sound admirable, but unless those qualities are tempered with tolerance and compassion, they're only superiority in disguise." He gave a rueful chuckle. "Luckily I have a sister who likes to remind me of my shortcomings."

"Well, thank you for the apology. It means a lot." She managed to raise her gaze. "I want you to know I wish you and Patricia all the best."

A flush spread across his cheeks, and he opened his mouth to speak.

But she turned away, not wanting to hear about his new relationship. She picked up the decorated box and held it out to him. "You'd better get going. Maxi will be waiting."

Aidan took the box, and then set it back on the counter. "Chloe, wait. There is no Patricia and me."

"What do you mean? The kids told me you were…together now."

His eyebrows drew into a frown. "We've gone out

to dinner a few times, but as friends. I promise you there is nothing romantic between us."

Chloe fought for equilibrium as she tried to process what he was telling her. Her heart pumped so hard against her ribcage she could scarcely breathe.

Aidan captured one of her hands. "I've missed you so much," he said in a husky voice. "Can you ever forgive my stubborn pride?"

She swallowed the tears burning her throat. "There's nothing to forgive, Aidan. I only wish I hadn't hurt you."

"I know." With one finger, he tipped her head up to stare into her eyes. "I love you, Chloe. And if you'll let me, I'll spend the rest of my life trying to make it up to you."

Joy and disbelief leapt in her veins. *Aidan loved her?*

His eyes searched hers, waiting for her reply.

On a sigh, she reached up to cup his face and drew him closer. When his lips met hers, her eyes fluttered closed, and she drank in his familiar taste, reveling in the scent of his aftershave and the hint of stubble that brushed her jaw. His arms tightened around her as he returned the kiss with equal measure.

When they finally drew apart, Aidan gave her a hopeful look. "Does this mean you'll give me another chance?"

She nodded, a slow smile blooming. "I love you too, Aidan. I promise to be a better person for you."

"You're perfect just the way you are. I'm the one who needed to change. And thanks to you, I have."

She fought to contain the rush of emotions that tumbled through her. "I—I don't know what to say. This is all so unexpected."

He grinned at her apparent bewilderment. "For starters, say you'll come to the official unveiling of the youth center's new sign. It'll be a fun night." He sobered. "We've missed you being there."

Chloe blinked back happy tears. She'd hated avoiding the center, but it brought back too many painful memories of her time with Aidan.

"Which reminds me," he continued. "I need to order a cake—a very large cake—for the celebration." He tugged her back against his chest. "I hear there's a fabulous new bakery in town where I can get one made."

Floating on a wave of pure joy, she laughed. "I don't know if you can afford my prices, Mr. North. Custom-made cakes that size are pretty expensive."

"Hmm. Well, now that I'm kissing the cook, maybe I can get a discount. In fact," he moved his lips to her ear, "I'm hoping to make it a lifetime discount."

Shivers coursed down Chloe's arms. She looked into his eyes, amazed to find them shining with love. "Nothing would make me happier."

And when he kissed her again, Chloe gave silent thanks for the miracle of second chances.

EPILOGUE

One month later

"I pronounce *Aspirations*, the Rainbow Falls Youth Center, officially opened." Aidan pulled the rope and the black cloth fell away.

A loud cheer went up from the crowd gathered outside the building.

Chloe clapped so hard her hands hurt.

Aidan had put off the official opening until the new sign could be installed.

She blinked back tears of happiness at the joy on Matt's face as he took in his prize-winning title captured in bold black letters above the doorway. She thanked God for the millionth time at the changes she'd witnessed in this boy.

Aidan quieted the crowd in preparation for the little speech he'd rehearsed—the one he wouldn't let her hear in advance.

"I want to thank everyone for coming today. This center means a lot to me and, I hope, to the youth of this town. Together we can do great things, not only for ourselves, but for our community, with the many outreach projects we have planned." He paused while everyone applauded. "There is one person to whom I owe a huge debt of thanks, and that is Miss Chloe Martin. Without her support and enthusiasm, this center would never have taken off the way it has."

The group broke into wild applause.

A flush heated Chloe's cheeks.

"I also want to thank Chloe for another wonderful thing…" He paused, grinning at her. "For agreeing to become my wife."

Someone let out a loud wolf-whistle.

Chloe laughed as more applause followed. A bubble of pure joy rose in her chest, threatening to lift her feet from the ground.

"So hopefully the next time a crowd this big gets together, it will be at the Good Shepherd Church for our wedding."

A murmur of laughter rippled through the group.

"Now let's go inside and continue the celebration with cake and punch."

Aidan opened the doors, and the people herded inside, their happy chatter drifting inward.

Chloe smiled at all the congratulatory remarks and pats on the shoulder as everyone moved past her. When only she and Aidan remained outside, she turned to him with a smile, her heart expanding with love. "That was some speech, Mr. North."

"Glad you liked it." He brushed a kiss across her lips. "I forgot one thing though." He reached inside his jacket and pulled out a small, blue velvet box. With a flick, he opened the lid to reveal a marquise-cut diamond. "I know you accepted my proposal, but I'd like to make it official."

"Oh, Aidan. It's stunning." She threw her arms around his neck and kissed him, not caring who might see them. "I love you, and I can't wait to start our life together."

Aidan's gray eyes darkened. "Thank you for saving me from myself, Chloe. Without you, I'd have turned into a grumpy old man."

Chloe laughed. "You were a bit uptight as I recall." Still standing on her tiptoes, she tilted her head. "There is something I've always wondered though."

"What's that?" His fingers caressed her cheek, adding to the warmth of the sun on her shoulders.

"Why were you so mean to me when we were teens?"

"I wasn't mean."

"You don't remember making fun of me in front of your friends?"

A flush stole up his neck. "Oh, that."

"Yes, that."

He loosened his collar with one finger. "I couldn't very well admit that I had a crush on my little sister's friend, could I?" He shrugged. "So I made fun of you instead."

Chloe's mouth fell open. "You had a crush on me back then?"

He grinned. "What can I say? I had a thing for klutzy girls with braces."

She smacked his arm, pretending outrage.

"Who knew that klutzy girl would literally knock me off my feet one rainy night." His eyes danced with laughter. "You've been knocking me off balance ever since."

She laughed with him, and as images of her extended family came to mind, she thanked God for giving her the one thing she'd craved since growing up an only child—a big, noisy family. God had brought Lily into her life several years ago, and now, by marrying Aidan, Maxi would become her sister, as well as her friend, and Bernice would fill the hole left by her mother's death.

Chloe caressed the locket around her neck, certain

both her birth mother and the woman who'd raised her would be very proud of her now. God had used Matt and Lindsay Brown, as well as the amazing man at her side, as instruments of redemption, blessing her with the hope of salvation.

With a happy sigh, she held out her left hand. "Don't just stand there, Mr. North. Put that ring on and let's get started on our future."

"With pleasure, Miss Martin. With pleasure."

He slipped the ring on her finger, and then his lips sealed the deal in a most satisfying manner.

Thank you

We appreciate you reading this White Rose Publishing title. For other inspirational stories, please visit our on-line bookstore at www.pelicanbookgroup.com.

For questions or more information, contact us at customer@pelicanbookgroup.com.

White Rose Publishing
Where Faith is the Cornerstone of Love™
an imprint of Pelican Book Group
www.PelicanBookGroup.com

Connect with Us
www.facebook.com/Pelicanbookgroup
www.twitter.com/pelicanbookgrp

To receive news and specials, subscribe to our bulletin
http://pelink.us/bulletin

May God's glory shine through
this inspirational work of fiction.

AMDG

You Can Help!

At Pelican Book Group it is our mission to entertain readers with fiction that uplifts the Gospel. It is our privilege to spend time with you awhile as you read our stories.

We believe you can help us to bring Christ into the lives of people across the globe. And you don't have to open your wallet or even leave your house!

Here are 3 simple things you can do to help us bring illuminating fiction™ to people everywhere.

1) If you enjoyed this book, write a positive review. Post it at online retailers and websites where readers gather. And share your review with us at reviews@pelicanbookgroup.com (this does give us permission to reprint your review in whole or in part.)

2) If you enjoyed this book, recommend it to a friend in person, at a book club or on social media.

3) If you have suggestions on how we can improve or expand our selection, let us know. We value your opinion. Use the contact form on our web site or e-mail us at customer@pelicanbookgroup.com

God Can Help!

Are you in need? The Almighty can do great things for you. Holy is His Name! He has mercy in every generation. He can lift up the lowly and accomplish all things. Reach out today.

> *Do not fear: I am with you; do not be anxious: I am your God. I will strengthen you, I will help you, I will uphold you with My victorious right hand.*
> ~Isaiah 41:10 (NAB)

We pray daily, and we especially pray for everyone connected to Pelican Book Group—that includes you! If you have a specific need, we welcome the opportunity to pray for you. Share your needs or praise reports at http://pelink.us/pray4us

Free Book Offer

We're looking for booklovers like you to partner with us! Join our team of influencers today and receive at least one free eBook per month. Maybe more!

For more information
Visit http://pelicanbookgroup.com/booklovers